# Nibbled To Death By Ducks

**Books by Robert Campbell**

*Alice in La-La Land*
*Nibbled to Death by Ducks*
*Plugged Nickel*
*Red Cent*

Published by POCKET BOOKS

# NIBBLED TO DEATH BY DUCKS

## Robert Campbell

**POCKET BOOKS**

New York   London   Toronto   Sydney   Tokyo

POCKET BOOKS, a division of Simon & Schuster Inc.
1230 Avenue of the Americas, New York, NY 10020

ISBN: 0-671-67585-0

First Pocket Books Trade Hardcover Printing November 1989

10  9  8  7  6  5  4  3  2  1

POCKET and colophon are trademarks of
Simon & Schuster Inc.

Printed in the U.S.A.

*For Rob . . .*
*who wants to be a writer . . .*
*who is a writer.*

# 1

My wife's name is Mary Ellen. I used to call her by both names when we was first living together. Now that we're married I call her Mary.

My old man's name is Mike.

Mary's mother is Charlotte and her aunt, Charlotte's sister, is Sada.

The kid what lives next door is Stanley Recore and the sister and brother what own the grocery store downstairs are Pearl and Joe Pakula.

Chips Delvin, my Chinaman—which is like what the New York cops call a rabbi—is actually Francis Brendan Delvin. He gave me my start in the Chicago sewers and Democratic politics. His housekeeper is Mrs. Banjo.

There's a lot you can learn from names and the way people use them.

For instance, my whole name is James Barnabas Flannery, but only my mother—God rest her soul—and Mary ever call me James. My old man calls me Jim. Most people call me Jimmy. One or two call me Jimbo when they want to give me the curly lip. Nobody has ever called me Barnabas or Barney, and nobody ever will if I got anything to say about it.

My wife works as a nurse over to Passavant Hospital. It's a very stressful profession. Which is not to say she complains about it very often. It's just that when she gets quieter and quieter and doesn't take too much kidding around I know it's time she should take a break.

I manage to convince her she ain't indispensable to every one of her patients, and we take off for a week's vacation down to New Orleans, a town which she's never seen and I only been to once for about a day and a half myself.

I can tell you everything we did down there, but I won't since this ain't a travelogue. I'll just say it rained five out of the seven days, but we had a very good time all the same.

It's when we get back that we find out things ain't so good since we left.

The taxi leaves us off downstairs, and we climb the six flights to the third floor with our suitcases. Mike, who's been staying in our place so he can take care of Alfie, my dog, opens the door before I have to use my key.

"You have a good time?" he asks.

"It rained a lot," I says.

"That's the way it is all the time down there in New Orleans."

"How do you know? You never been," I says, putting down the suitcases and getting a lick from Alfie after he finishes giving the big hello to Mary.

"Everybody knows it's always raining in New Orleans."

"We had a good time, Mike," Mary says, giving him a kiss on the cheek and stopping what she figures is going to be an argument over nothing.

"Anyway, who cares," Mike says. "There's other things more important."

"Something the matter?"

"It's Delvin."

"He ain't dead, is he?" I blurt out, having the feeling that what I expected was going to happen for the last year or so finally happens.

"No, that much's all right," Mike says.

"Is he sick again?"

"I suppose you could say that, though it's none of the ailments that've put him to bed before."

I notice that my father, like a lot of people when they grow old, is falling into the habit of taking one hell of a long time to deliver a joke, a story, or a piece of news.

"Well, are you going to tell us or ain't you going to tell us?"

"You shouldn't be in such a hurry to hear the worst," Mike says.

"I'm just trying to find out what the worst is."

"Delvin's suffered a great loss. It knocked him flat."

"A great loss of what?"

"Mrs. Banjo. She passed away sudden the day after you left."

It hits me very hard, what he says.

"I'll make some tea," Mary says.

It's not that there was any great affection between Mrs. Banjo and me. At least none that I ever thought about until just this second. I mean she was Delvin's housekeeper for I don't know how many years—ever since his wife died—but every time I appeared on the doorstep she always acted as if she wasn't sure if I was all that welcome, even when I'd been invited. She'd usually scold me for standing in the doorway wiping my feet and letting in the cold air or not wearing my galoshes if it was wet out or sneezing in the hallway if I had a cold. She'd bring in lemonades or hot toddies—depending on the weather—laced with whiskey, knowing that I didn't drink, and Delvin, who shouldn't've had more than one, would have mine as well. After delivering the refreshments she'd go to some other part of the house, and that's the last I'd see of her.

"You better sit down," Mike says.

I go into the kitchen and sit down at the table, afraid that I'm going to cry and not knowing why.

The kettle starts to sing.

"What took her?" I asks.

"Heart failure. In her bed during the night," Mike says. "From the look of her, Delvin said, she went very quiet, and he hopes he'll do the same."

"How old a woman was she?" Mary asks.

"I don't know," I says.

Mike sits down on the other side of the table, running his hand over the oilcloth as though taking comfort from it.

"She was seventy-five if she was a day," he says.

"How's that?" I says, startled. "She couldn't've been that old. Her hair was black as jet, and she had arms on her like a docker."

"Oh, she was a sturdy woman sure enough, but the color of her hair came out of a bottle."

"She's been waked already, has she?" I asks.

"Waked and blessed and buried," Mike says.

"You should've sent me word. I could've come home for the funeral."

"What good would it've done her?"

"It would've done old Delvin good."

"You weren't unrepresented, Jim. After all, I was there."

Mary sets down a cup of tea for each of us and goes back to the stove.

"He ask about me?" I says.

"Once or twice," Mike says. "I explained that you were off taking a little vacation."

"What'd he say to that?"

Mike acts like he's reluctant to say.

"Go on," I says, "you ain't going to hurt my feelings."

"Well, he grumped—you know the way he does—and says it ain't surprising you wouldn't be there when he needed you."

I don't say anything, but I think to myself that's just like old Delvin, taking the chance to give me the needle even though I helped him out of more bad scrapes than I can count. Come to think of it, maybe that's why he takes these little shots at me. Because he figures he's like the grandfather and I'm just a kid compared to him, so it bothers him that I've saved his bacon more than once.

"But mostly he acts dazed," my father goes on. "Like he's lost most of his fire."

"Well, he'll stoke it up again, you can bet on that," I says. But I'm not sure I really believe it.

Mary comes over and sits down at the table with a cup of tea for herself.

"Do you think it's too late for you to call up Mr. Delvin, James?" she asks.

I glance up at the kitchen clock. It ain't yet ten.

I start to stand up, but Mike says, "It wouldn't be too late to call the old man if he was home, but he ain't."

"Where is he, then?"

"He's at a facility what closes off incoming calls at nine o'clock."

"Facility?"

"For the last three days he's been in a nursing home by the name of the Larkspur over to the Fourteenth Ward."

"The Fourteenth? He hates the Fourteenth ever since Hilda Moscowitz beat out George Lurgan for alderman. You'd have to drag him out of his house biting and kicking to get him over there."

"He didn't have any fight left in him," Mike says. "Mrs. Banjo's dying took the last bit of starch out of him. He just about collapsed at the graveside. Wally Dunleavy and this other fella got him into the limousine. The next thing I heard was that Delvin was in this nursing home."

"I don't believe he'd leave his house without a fight."

"I was told he went without hardly a murmur," Mike says.

"Temporary shock," I says. "He was brain-stunned from grief. Any minute now that phone'll ring, and it'll be Delvin asking me how come I ain't over there taking him home like he'd be doing for me if our situations was reversed."

Well, we sit there until almost midnight, and the phone never rings.

# 2

The next morning I look up the address and telephone number of the Larkspur Nursing Home while Mary's getting ready to go to work and Mike's making breakfast.

"You going over to see Delvin this morning?" Mike asks.

"As soon as I have a cup of coffee," I says.

"You want me to come along?"

"I'd just as soon see him the first time on my own."

"You could be right. But I want to warn you again, Jim, he's not the man he was."

"You've been to see him?"

"Of course I have." He hesitates again, like he did last night, and then he says, "I scarcely recognized him, though."

"Grief can change a man's looks."

"What was worse, I don't think he recognized me."

I decide I don't want to hear any more before I see for myself how Delvin's doing.

Mary takes the car, so I grab the A train to Sixty-third and Racine. It's about eight blocks to Sherman Park, and then about a mile and a half west to the Larkspur, which is on a street right by Micek Pig Park, practically sitting on the Baltimore and Ohio Central railroad just north of a switching yard.

For those of you what don't live in Chicago, I could mention that there's these little playground parks all over the city, squares of open space and some grass with a sandbox and a jungle gym and a slide and maybe some telephone poles stuck in the ground for the kiddies to climb around and sit on. There's some swings and, for a minute, I think how nice it'd be to take a swing, but I keep going.

The nursing home looks pretty good from the outside with the sprinklers going, watering a lawn that ain't too patchy. There's a whole bunch of delphiniums against the latticework around the porch.

It's a huge old three-story converted mansion, maybe one of the last ones still surviving in the neighborhood, with towers that go up another story topping off both wings.

It's got broad side yards bordered with privet twenty feet high, all nicely trimmed and shaped. I walk over, dodging the sprinklers, and peek around the back. Once there was nothing but big back yards around here, and this one goes all the way to a stand of trees on the other street. The only other house I passed along the way with a yard this big was another old mansion somebody'd turned into a funeral home.

In front of the trees there's a couple of stone benches and a little pond. I hear some ducks quacking, so I take the path around the house and have a look.

The pond ain't natural, though I can't see the pipe for the water coming in or the drain where it's going out. The water's pretty clear, so I know it's moving, or maybe they clean it out every once in a while. Anyway, there's a dozen ducks lying around on the grass or swimming around in the pond enjoying themselves, quacking away like a bunch of people on a picnic. I don't know if the Larkspur stocks the pond with these ducks or if they're city ducks what spotted the pond when they was flying around and decided it was better than any of the big ponds in some of the other parks. It's a very pleasant spot, and I start feeling a little better about Delvin being there.

I go around to the front and walk up the steps to the porch.

There's five or six rocking chairs sitting on it, but nobody's in them. People don't sit on porches taking the air the way they used to. Television put the kibosh on that. It's hard for me to understand sometimes why so many people would rather watch faces talking at one another on a nineteen-inch screen than visit with their neighbors or even any strangers passing by, but that's the way things are nowadays.

When I step inside the reception area I can see this big living room with an enclosed porch off to one side. There's maybe half a dozen old folks sitting there in these high chairs with wheels, staring at a color television set that has got to be one of them forty-inch projection jobs.

The place looks very nice and pleasant, what with long lace curtains at the windows and flowered slipcovers on all the chairs and couches.

There's a big vase full of fresh flowers on a long desk, which is the only thing that reminds you this ain't a private home anymore. That and the old people staring at the television, of course.

There's nobody sitting behind the desk, but I notice one of them little bells like they got in hotels sitting on it, so I go over and give it a tap. Somebody out on the porch lets out a yelp, and somebody else laughs. I suppose me ringing the bell is more excitement than they've had in a month of Sundays.

There's a wooden box full of old slippers and shoes next to the door marked "Private," which is next to a door marked "Office."

While I'm looking at that I hear somebody yell, "Mama, Mama, they won't let me out!" from somewhere way down the hall. "Bring me a saw so I can make a hole! Mama, Mama, if you get me out, I'll be a good girl forever!"

It gives me the chills.

Then whoever it is lets out a scream fit to wake the dead and starts crying, "Oh, oh, oh, oh, oh, you're keeping me prisoner against my will. When my husband, Jake, finds out what you're doing to me he'll come kill each and every one of you. You, too, Peter Rabbit. You, too."

I'm halfway down the hall while she's yelling all this. Whenever I hear somebody yelling for help or sounding like they're in pain, I always go to see if there's anything I can do, though some people accuse me of sticking my nose in where it don't belong and I should learn to mind my own business.

It seems to me, because people are so worried about sticking their nose in and minding their own business, it's got so a person's not safe on the streets anymore. You could be getting robbed in broad daylight or stabbed to death by a maniac on State Street, and the crowds would just walk on by, keeping their noses straight ahead and their minds on their own business.

I follow my nose and my ears down the long main corridor to a side hall that has got a stairway at the end of it. It sounds to me like the voice is coming from up on the second floor, the stairwell acting like a megaphone, spreading the noise all over the place.

"Oh, you bastards," she cries out. "Oh, you bastards."

I take the stairs two at a time and hit the hallway on the second floor running. I get closer and closer to the woman who's yelling. A lot of other people are yelling now, too, their cries adding to the racket.

I stop in front of an open door where two female orderlies are tying an old woman about ninety down to the bed with restraints. The smell hits me like a wet diaper right in the face. The old woman's half out of her nightgown, and it ain't a pleasant sight.

She spots me and says, "What took you so long, Jake? Shoot these fucking whores. Shoot them between the fucking eyes." Then she lets go a stream of filthy language what would bring a Chicago cop to his knees.

One of the orderlies, a pleasant-looking Latino girl with a round face and soft brown eyes, looks over her shoulder at me and smiles.

"Ain' she got a mouth?" she says. "Would you believe? Her husband was a minister."

"Jake?"

"So she say. So she say."

"Aeschrolalia," somebody says behind me.

I turn around to face this chunky young woman wearing a tailored gray two-piece suit with a white ruffled blouse and a little striped necktie. She shoots her cuffs like a man would do, then touches her hair to see that the bun didn't come undone.

"What?" I says.

She's got a hand under my elbow, steering me out of the doorway and down the hall. "Aeschrolalia. The compulsive, involuntary use of filthy language. It's an aberration that manifests itself in certain psychotic patients."

"You got mental cases in here?" I says.

"We've got all kinds. Ever since the state closed down a great many of their mental facilities, the cities and counties have felt the impact. I was an intern in a—"

"You're a doctor?"

"No, I was doing a management internship in a nursing home in Old Town back in the seventies when the mental homes shut down. They delivered people as bad as that and worse to the nursing homes by the busload. Now would you mind telling me who you are and what you're doing wandering around?"

By this time she's got me maneuvered all the way down the hall and halfway down the stairs. She touches the bun at the back of her neck again.

"Your hair looks fine," I says, figuring to do what I can to get things on a better footing.

She blushes, which makes her blue eyes look even bluer, and smiles. "Irish, are you?"

"How could you tell?"

"Well, besides the red hair and fair complexion, you're quick to compliment a woman."

"Why not? It cheers a person up."

"I could use a little cheering up."

"Can I help?"

"That's what I'm supposed to say to you."

"I come to visit a friend who was admitted last week."

"What would the name be?"

"Delvin."

"Oh, yes, Frank."

Nobody ever calls Chips Delvin "Frank," so her trying to act like she's already very friendly with him ain't very convincing.

"That would be him," I says.

"He was admitted in a very morose and subdued state of mind."

"I suppose that's to be expected under the circumstances, ain't it?"

"He lost a relative, didn't he?"

"A friend of long standing."

"At his age he must lose several every year," she says, as though anybody what reaches a certain age should expect to see his friends drop off like flies and not care—at least not complain—about it.

"I think he's already outlived most of the friends he ever had," I says. "I mean old friends that he could share the old stories with. I could be among the last."

"Aren't you too young to be an old friend?" she says, smearing a little of my own butter back on me. She could maybe even be flirting with me a little.

"I mean I'm maybe one of the oldest he's got left," I says. "He was like my teacher. He taught me most of what I know."

"About what, Mr. . . . ?"

"Flannery. Jimmy Flannery. About politics and the sewer system, Ms. . . . ?"

"Evergreen. Lenore Evergreen. So, do you work for the city, then?"

"Just like Mr. Delvin, who's give a lifetime to it. Could I see him now?"

She hesitates for a second. I can see that she's thinking about just telling me no flat out. But I also see that she knows I'm not the sort of man to take no for an answer without wanting to know the reason why. So she takes the path of least resistance and says, "He's probably asleep. He was exhausted from the rigors of the funeral. Exhausted and disoriented."

"That happened almost a week ago."

"The very old don't always recover as quickly as we might hope. They can go on for years, losing people and bouncing back like rubber balls. Then they lose one too many, and they drift off on a sea of forgetfulness."

All of which sounds very melancholy, very poetic even, but I figure that with a tough old bird like Delvin it's more likely that without Mrs. Banjo there to scold him for taking more than one glass of whiskey, or two at most, he'd had too much to drink at the wake. That's what made him too weak to fight against being trucked off to a nursing home and too weak to get the hell out of bed and go home the next day or the day after that. Now, after nearly a week in a strange place, he should be raising hell to get out of here and back to his living room, even if he had the worst hangover in the history of the world.

A big black man wearing track pants with a white jacket over a sweat shirt comes through a side door and starts walking away from us, down toward the lobby, as we reach the bottom of the stairs and the main corridor.

I take a gander at Evergreen's face as it tightens up like a fist. "Robert," she says in a voice that cracks like a whip.

He stops in his tracks, turns around, and comes trotting back to us.

He's got this respectful look on his face that ain't really respectful, if you know what I mean. It's like a cartoon drawing of respectful. Respectful or otherwise, it's a face I wouldn't want to meet in a dark alley. Or even one that was all lit up, for that matter. There's a scar running down one side of his face from eyebrow to chin, with a little side trip to the corner of his lip which lifts it up like he's ready to snarl.

"You know you're never to leave the front desk unattended," Evergreen says.

"Ma'am, I try to fin' somebody to relieve me while I go to relieve myself," he says, in this accent that goes up and down like he's singing, "but there be nobody hear me, an' I go do wha' I got to do, otherwise I do it where I sit like some of dese ole folks."

"All right. All right," she says, waving him on and turning her back to him.

He gives me a wink over her head and a grin that shows more white teeth than I ever see in a man's mouth before. Then he pivots on one foot and takes a long stride away from us.

"Couldn't you come back later in the day?" Evergreen says. "The mornings are really very busy. Besides, visiting hours don't really start until two o'clock."

"Well, with him just being admitted within the last few days and all, can't we bend the rules a little just this once?"

"We have to have a routine in order to get the work done."

"I understand that. I could go sit out on a bench in Micek Park if you want."

"You'd have to sit there for four hours. I'm sure you've got better things to do," she says, like she suspects that since I got a job with the city I probably got nothing to do at all.

"Well, I just came back into town from a trip to New Orleans, and I'm pretty determined to explain to my old friend why I wasn't there when he needed me. You understand that this's very important to me."

I was being reasonable, and it's very hard to say no to a man who's being reasonable. Especially one who looks to be stubborn, too.

But she's also ready to be stubborn.

"It's a nice morning," she says, "and if you've got the time, I suppose sitting on a bench in the park isn't the worst thing you could do for four hours. I'll show you out," she says. "I wouldn't want you to lose your way."

There's nothing I can do but go along unless I want to start a fight, and I got no reason to do that.

We turn the corner into the main corridor.

Down at the end there's an orderly in a white coat raising his hand to an old man wearing the jacket to a pin-striped business suit over his hospital gown.

The old man's skinny legs are so white they're almost blue, and his feet're swimming around in a pair of scuffed wing tips without laces.

Neither one of them sees or hears us.

"Why do you hate me?" the old man asks in this quavering voice.

"You want to know why I hate you?" the orderly says. "I hate you because you're old and you stink and because I told you fifty times you can't wear your suit because you're not going any-where."

He raises his hand a little higher like he's going to hit the old man. Evergreen gasps and I says, "Hey, you!"

"Just a moment, Mr. Flannery. This has nothing to do with you," Evergreen says, but she's saying it to my back because I'm already halfway from here to there.

The orderly turns around and drops his arm into a better position for punching me when I get close enough, because I guess it looks to him like I'm on the attack.

"Jack!" Evergreen hollers, and he looks confused.

I reach around him and take the old man's arm to get him out of harm's way. It scares him. He don't know who I am, and he don't know but what I could be just somebody new going to give him a hard time. I hear Evergreen's shoes tap-tapping on the linoleum as she runs toward us.

Before anything goes any further she's got her arm around the old man's shoulders, soothing him and crooning that everything's going to be all right.

"I just wanted to stop in at the office," the old man says.

"I know that, Mr. Custer, but Jack didn't know that. He was just following orders trying to get you back to your room."

"He hates me," Custer says. "He said so."

"He might get exasperated when you run away from him like you do, Mr. Custer, but I doubt he hates you," she says. "That's just his way of getting over the fright you gave him."

She's very good at calming him down. In a minute she hands him over to Jack, who's all of a sudden all peaches and cream, and he helps the old man along the hall as gentle as you please.

He opens the door to a room and lets Mr. Custer go inside first, then follows him, closing the door very carefully like he's trying to show us what an easygoing man he is.

Evergreen looks at me and says, "Are you around old people very much?"

"Not that old."

"How old?"

"Well, my father's in his sixties."

She smiles and asks, "He ever get on your nerves losing things? Being forgetful or stubborn?"

"Sometimes."

She nods like she's saying well, there you are, don't be so critical of the way some of us lose our tempers a little now and then.

"But I wouldn't raise my hand to him," I says.

"Jack Boxer was threatening Mr. Custer like you'd threaten a child."

"Boxer? That his name? It suits him. I wouldn't go around threatening a child. Is that the way you do nowadays?"

"I'm not defending what Jack did. I'm merely explaining. He's got a short temper sometimes, but Jack would never actually hit a patient."

Well, I don't know about that, I says to myself. Somebody thinks it's okay to threaten a kid or an old person with a slap, it's as good as slapping them, it seems to me. And you raise your hand often enough, one day you're just going to let go.

"Mr. Custer's in his nineties," Evergreen says, "incontinent and senile. Once we found him walking down the avenue two blocks away. He was wearing a shirt, tie, and the jacket to his suit. He wasn't wearing his trousers or any underpants. We confine him to his room as much as we can since then."

"He got any relatives come to take him out of here on a little excursion now and then?"

"He has a couple of children. Both on in years and not too well themselves. Grandchildren. They came often at first. Took him home at Easter, Christmas, and on his birthday. They don't do that anymore. He's too hard to manage. They pay for his care. They convince themselves that's all they have to do. After all, half the time he didn't even know them when they did come to visit."

By this time she's walked me all the way to the front door. The black man's sitting at the desk as we go by, and he grins at me again.

Evergreen opens the door for me and walks me all the way out to the top of the porch steps.

"You know where the park is?" she asks, very helpful and all.

"Don't worry, I'll find it," I says.

"I'm sorry I couldn't break the rules for you, Mr. Flannery."

"I'll just go take care of some things and come back."

"So you'll be back at two?"

"I'll be back," I says as I walk down the steps and out along the path. I look back once. Evergreen's watching me with a look on her face of somebody who's under a lot of pressure and at the end of her rope.

I walk down to the corner, then turn left and go down one block, then left again to the stand of trees behind the nursing home. I stand there hidden by the trees, just on the other side of the duck pond, and watch the back of the house until I figure there's nobody looking out of any of the windows what could see me. Then I hurry across the grass to a basement door.

I don't think it's a door that's used much because there's leaves piled up against the sill and there's a padlock on it. I take out my nail file.

This kid, Stanley Recore, what talks funny and lives across the hall from Mary and me, shows me once how to open just about any kind of common lock. Padlocks is the easiest next to them useless little locks they got on briefcases and suitcases.

I stick the tip of the file into the keyhole and jiggle it around a little bit until it snaps open. I take the lock off and put it into my pocket.

The basement smells of coal dust from the days before natural gas or heating oil. The bins where the coal used to be kept is loaded with old luggage and furniture. All the other storage space, which is surrounded by lath partitions, is full of old furniture, too. The rest of the cellar, which looks like a big cave, accommodates a couple of big furnaces that are dead and another, smaller one, which is burning. That's the one that probably heats the huge boiler that provides the hot water.

There's more than one staircase leading to the first floor.

I stand there, recalling the floor plan of the house above my head, until I calculate which staircase'll get me into the corridor where old Mr. Custer has his room.

The door at the top of the stairs is locked. There's no Yale or Chubb on it, just a regular old-fashioned keyhole lock you could open with a skeleton key—which I happen to have a couple of on my key ring that a friend of mine, Jim Trupin, give me. I take a peek through the keyhole before I unlock the door with the blank key.

There's nobody in the hallway. I cross over to Mr. Custer's door and tap on it while I'm trying the knob. The door's locked.

"Who's that?" he asks from inside, the second time I do it. I can hardly hear him.

I want him to come closer so I don't have to speak above a whisper, so I tap on the door again, which gets him over next to it on the other side.

"Who is it?" he says again.

"I'm the guy what came over and tried to help you when Jack was yelling at you a little while ago."

"Oh. You sure?"

"Sure, I'm sure."

"Then let me thank you, sir."

"You could do me a favor," I says.

He don't reply, and I figure he's afraid I'm going to ask him to do something that'll get him into trouble.

"It's nothing much," I says. "Nothing that'll get you in any trouble as long as we keep it between you and me."

"Something secret?"

"Well, not secret exactly, but something we'll just keep to ourselves."

I can tell he's thinking that one over, like maybe here's a chance to show a little rebellion, a little independence, without jumping into a tub of hot water.

"Tell me what the favor is," he says. "If it means going anywhere, I can't help you, because they've taken my clothes and locked me in."

"I just want you to give me a little information."

"That's all right, then. I can do that if I know what it is you want."

"You know Mr. Delvin? Francis Delvin?"

"You mean Chips?"

"That's right."

"Yes, we met once, but we couldn't talk much because he's not been feeling very well."

"You happen to know where his room is?"

"Two doors down the hall toward the back."

"Thanks."

"So, what's the favor you want me to do for you?"

"That's it."

"What's the secret?" he asks, his voice getting a little louder and sounding kind of desperate, like I'm going to leave before I tell him what the secret is.

I got to give him a secret or I don't know but what he might start shouting and bring somebody running.

"The secret is that I'm investigating this establishment and I'd like you to keep an eye on this guy, Jack Boxer, for me," I says, making it up on the spur of the moment. "Can you do that?"

"What do you want me to look for?"

"I want you to count the number of times he raises his voice or his hand to anybody like he did to you."

There's a pause, and then he says, "Do I have to be an eyewitness to the incident?"

"Hearsay's okay as long as the person who tells you about it's trustworthy."

"I'll do my best," he says.

"Two doors down, you said, right?"

"That's right. Two doors back. Same side of the hall."

"Thanks again," I says, and I straighten up from where I'm stooping by the door with my head practically up against it.

I go down two rooms and open the door without bothering to knock.

The drapes are closed and the room's dark. I smell some sort of medication, but I can't tell what. The rest of what I smell ain't so good either. There's a big mound what could be Delvin lying on the bed under the covers.

"Mr. Delvin?" I says in a voice just a breath above a whisper.

He don't move. I go over and open the curtains.

The room ain't the prettiest I ever seen. The floor's dirty and there's some kind of stains on the wall like somebody threw a cup of coffee or something at it and let it run down and dry.

The person in the bed turns over and pushes the blanket away.

I go take a peek. It's Delvin all right.

The blanket looks old and the sheets and pillowcases look like they ain't been washed lately.

I look at him laying there on his back, breathing through his mouth, his chin shoveled down on his bony chest, his white hair lying like old lint across his skull. He's so pale his freckles and liver marks look like spatters of brown paint.

I sit down in the chair next to the bed, lean over, and say his name a few times. He stirs a little and half opens his eyes to look at me, but they don't focus, and he closes them right away. I find one of his hands under the blankets and hold it to let him know I'm there. It's like I'm holding a bundle of twigs.

"It's Jimmy Flannery, Mr. Delvin. I come to tell to you I'm here if you need me."

He pushes out his lips and makes a noise like steam escaping from a radiator valve. I don't know does that mean he's glad, sad, or mad.

"You sign yourself in here, Mr. Delvin, or did somebody do this to you?" I asks.

He mumbles and grumbles. His eyelids flutter. But that's all I can get out of him.

I sit there for maybe ten minutes, and then I leave and go out through the cellar the way I came, replacing the lock and making sure nobody's out in the back yard or by the pond when I cross the lawn, heading for the trees.

When I get there I look back at the Larkspur. Somebody's standing in one of the second floor windows watching me. At first it gives me a start because now I'm worried somebody knows somebody was sneaking around. Then the person raises a hand, and I know it's Mr. Custer, watching out for things like I asked him to.

# 3

I grab a cab over to Passavant Hospital and get the keys to my car from Mary. I tell her I'll be back to pick her up at four-thirty.

"I can take the El," she says.

"No, I'll pick you up."

"If you can ride the El, I can ride the El," she says.

"I like to ride the El," I says. "You don't."

"So why do you need the car?"

"I got some running around to do."

"Like what?"

"Like I'm going over to the undertaker what buried Mrs. Banjo and see what I can find out about who helped Wally Dunleavy put Mr. Delvin into the limo after the graveside prayer. I think he could be the villain what signed Delvin into the nursing home. Then I'm going back over to the Larkspur and have a visit with the old man, and then—"

"I thought you were there to see him this morning."

"I was, but they said it wasn't visiting hours until two o'clock. Any time before that would upset their routine."

Mary nods her head as though confirming that a lot of health care facilities like to run their schedules that way.

"What kind of a place is it?" she asks.

"I don't know," I says, because I don't want to say what I think

about the accommodations until I know a little more. I got a bad
enough reputation for jumping to conclusions and going off
half-cocked as it is.

"Didn't you go inside?"

"Oh, sure, I went inside."

"So how did it look?"

"Nice curtains at the windows. Some old people in these high
chairs on wheels—"

"Geriatric chairs."

"—out on a side porch watching television. Carpets on the
floor."

Mary's nodding, a little pleased smile on her lips.

"At his age, all alone the way he is, maybe it's not such a bad idea
Mr. Delvin being cared for in a nice nursing home, James."

I'm about to tell her about the things that ain't so nice—half-
cocked or no half-cocked—when the dispatcher calls a code that
snaps Mary's head up. She gives me a quick kiss on the cheek,
turns, and hurries down the corridor.

"I'll get you at four-thirty," I call after her, and she waves her
hand in the air, telling me that's okay.

The drive over to Humphrey's Funeral Home on Union don't
take me more than twenty minutes.

Humphrey's is one of those old-fashioned undertakers the
old-timers still go to in droves, so there's almost always a full
house. Since they got six viewing rooms, that can make for
considerable complications as far as scheduling and parking goes.
But I never see a complication or a surprise old Dave Humphrey or
one of his six red-headed sons and daughters couldn't handle.

One of the daughters, Doreen, is sitting at the writing desk they
use for information and reception.

When we was kids we went to different high schools, but I met
her once at a football game in my junior year, and we sort of went
out together after that until we both graduated. Things got pretty
hot and heavy that summer, but then my mother—God rest her
soul—passed away from a cancer, and I got a job in the sewers and
moved over to the Twenty-seventh a couple of months after, and
somehow Doreen and me lost touch.

The only time I see her since is when I have to go to a funeral.

The first couple of times I walked in she gave me the sad face along with condolences on my loss of a loved one. When I told her they weren't people really close to me and that I was just fulfilling an obligation, she gave me the smile that used to curl my toes.

After the first couple of times she don't bother looking sad anymore but just grins at me and cracks wise about me stopping by to say good-bye to one of my constituents and how I probably write their names and birthdays down in my book so I shouldn't forget to vote them in the next election.

There's no modesty panel in front of the desk, and I'm standing there admiring her legs, which are still very good after ten years of marriage, three kids, and a divorce, when she looks up, sees me, and comes over with that big smile on her face. She gives me a little hug, nothing too bold considering where we are, and a little nuzzle alongside my ear.

"How's Mary keeping?" she says.

"Fine," I says.

"One of these days I've got to meet her. We can sit down and have a good old chat."

"About what?"

"About you, Jimmy Flannery."

"You do that and I could end up divorced or dead."

She gives this wicked little laugh, letting me know it's all in fun, and says, "Either way I'd have you for sure, Jimmy Flannery." Then she stops the kidding and asks me am I there seeing off a fellow Democrat.

"The person I should've seen off—God rest her soul—was buried while I was out of town."

"That would be a Mrs. Banjo, wouldn't it? I saw your father—a week ago Tuesday, was it?—at the funeral."

"That's about right."

"She was old man Delvin's housekeeper, wasn't she?"

"That's right. You know Chips Delvin?"

"We were introduced enough times at funerals for us to call each other by name. But you know how that is—undertakers and politicians are professional name collectors. It helps us earn our bread and butter, but it doesn't mean we know many people very well or ever even had much of a conversation with them."

A man and a woman come in and look around like they don't
know what to do or where to go. Doreen takes a step toward them.

"But you remember seeing him at Mrs. Banjo's laying out?" I
asks.

She turns her head, looking at the prospective customers, but
lays a hand on my arm to let me know she's still attending to what
I'm asking. "I was out of town until the day of the funeral. That's
when I saw your dad. I saw Mr. Delvin, too, very briefly, that same
day."

She raises her voice a little and says, "If you'll just take those
chairs by the desk, I'll be with you in a moment."

I put my hand over her hand, which is still on my sleeve.

"Did you see what happened at the graveside?"

"I wasn't there, but I heard tell that Mr. Delvin was taken badly
and that some relative stepped forward to take him in charge," she
says, looking at me again. "Maureen would know more about it.
She and Patrick went out to the cemetery, but she's the only one of
them working today. Shall I go get her?"

"Just point me the way."

"The Heather Room. It's over in the right-hand corner off the
small hall."

"I know where it is," I says.

"Stop at the desk and give me a kiss good-bye if I'm not busy,
will you?" she says, giving me a little bit of the twinkle and imp.
Then she puts on her respectful face and goes over to help the
couple.

I find my way to the Heather Room. Maureen, the oldest of the
three sisters, with a longer, sadder face than Doreen's, is bending
over a casket and tilting her head.

I come up alongside her, and she glances sideways at me and
says, "Hello, Jimmy. Here to pay your respects?"

"Belated," I says. "I was out of town when my friend, Mrs.
Banjo—God rest her soul—was laid out and buried from
here."

She looks at me with this thoughtful expression. "Do you know,
Jimmy, you're one of the few people I know says that anymore?"

"Says what?"

"God rest their soul. A few of the old people, perhaps, but I don't know a single person your age who says it anymore except for you."

"Maybe it'd be better if a few more started saying it again," I says.

"I was just thinking the same thing," she says, reaching over to arrange the hair along the cheek of the woman in the casket. Then she lifts the corpse's hands as casually as you'd lift a napkin and lets them drop into a more natural position on the woman's chest. "Better," Maureen says, stepping back. "Is there anything I can do for you, Jimmy?"

"Doreen tells me you was out to the cemetery when Mrs. Banjo was buried."

"That's right. Me and Patrick, I think."

"I'm told Mr. Delvin was took bad at the graveside."

"Overcome with grief or whatever."

"Whatever?"

"I think he may have sought the comfort of liquid refreshment to fortify himself before the funeral."

"What happened exactly?"

"Nothing very wrong. Nothing disgraceful. He just started crying, and his legs apparently grew weak. He would've fallen except there were people all around him. Two of them, Wally Dunleavy, the head of Streets and Sanitation—"

"Yes, I know."

"—and another big man, held him up and got him down the hillside and into the limousine."

"Did you know the other man?"

She turns her head away and thinks about it.

"It's on the tip of my tongue. I heard Dunleavy introduce him to someone during the laying out. Ah."

"Yes?"

"Carmody, it was. Francis Carmody."

I thank her and wave to Doreen on my way out. I don't stop to kiss her because she's still selling services.

I walk out to my car wondering who in the hell Francis Carmody might be.

# 4

I go down to the ward yard office over on West Madison in the Twenty-seventh where I have a desk. The same old scarred desk Delvin was sitting behind twenty years ago when I first laid eyes on him.

I done my duty and got in to see the old man, but I still don't feel like I done right by him. Maybe if he'd opened his eyes and looked at me like he knew me, or called me Jimbo like he does when he wants to take the mickey out of me, I could've gone on about my business feeling good. But the way he just lay there like he was waiting for the last tick of the clock made me feel very bad, so here I am trying to catch up on some paperwork but really waiting for two o'clock to roll around, sitting there thinking about how it all started between Delvin and me.

How I come down here where he hung out those days when I was just a kid and he was already an old man of sixty.

Not that he looked like an old man. He didn't. His hair—and he had plenty of it—was iron-gray and stiff as wire.

He looks me over and says, "So you're Mike Flannery's kid. I meet you before?"

"Once or twice, Mr. Delvin. I was a door knocker in the last election and did some hours stuffing envelopes down at party headquarters."

"Waste of money, that. Stuffing envelopes. Everybody knows

what the Democratic Party stands for." He grins this quick monkey grin at me. " 'Thou shalt not steal, but thou shalt not blow the whistle on anybody that does.' Ought to spend that money on old-fashioned smokers and family picnics. That's the way to run a campaign. You old enough to vote?"

"It won't be long."

"I took a look at your high-school record. You didn't do bad. How come you don't want to go on to college?"

I just shrug. What're you supposed to say when somebody asks you a question like that? You supposed to say there's nothing you can think of that you really want to do except get a decent job and maybe get married and have some kids down the road a ways? I was thinking maybe I could be a cop. Maybe I could be a fireman like my old man. The thing I really wanted to be was a precinct captain for the Democratic Party, which my father also was, but that ain't exactly a job with wages.

"I always figured I'd end up working for the city, one way or the other," I says.

"That ain't bad," Delvin says. "You like politics?"

"I like meeting people," I says.

"That's good. You understand favor for favor?"

"You know anybody in Chicago don't understand favor for favor?"

"You'll do, sonny," he says. "You ready to walk the sewers?"

"I didn't come here looking for a job in the sewers," I says. "Mike sent me down because I'm moving into the Twenty-seventh and he figures I should introduce myself to the ward leader."

"So you want to work for me and the party?"

"Yes, sir."

"That's good," he says again, like it's his favorite thing to say or the thing he says to buy some time while he thinks things over. "I can always use a good worker in the precincts. Keep your nose clean and you could be a captain someday. Right at the minute you got to have a job that pays a salary. So you'll walk the sewers. You ain't afraid of rats, are you?"

"I don't go jumping up on no tables when I see one."

"That's good," he says.

"That's good," he said way back then, and now he's lying on his back breathing through his mouth and I'm a precinct captain, sitting at his old desk in the ward yard, ready to step into his political shoes if I want them, though they ain't the shoes they was twenty years ago.

The hands on the clock hardly move, so I put the paperwork away and drive over to Micek Park, where I sit on a bench waiting for one-forty-five. Then I walk on over to the Larkspur again.

This time Lenore Evergreen comes out of her office the minute I walk into the lobby and says, "Well, you're back, Mr. Flannery."

"I said I would be."

"And you're a man of your word." There's a little edge to the way she says that. I don't know if she's trying to nail down in her mind what kind of a man I am or if she's being a little bit sarcastic. I let it breeze by.

She's walking down the main corridor, past the desk with the grinning black man sitting there giving me the eye, and I'm trotting behind her feeling like a customer following an usher down the aisle at a movie house.

She's smiling at me over her shoulder, and I'm smiling back.

She stops at a door halfway down the hall. It ain't the room I was in that morning. She knocks, opens it without waiting for a reply, and lets me go in by myself.

"Have a nice visit," she says, and she shuts the door behind her.

This room smells a lot better than the other one. At least somebody's aired it out, and the sheets on the bed look clean. The drapes are pulled back, and the sun's streaming through the window onto the tile floor, which looks like it was just scrubbed. There's some flowers in a green vase on the table by the window and a cheery print of some yellow ducks on the wall.

Delvin's in a clean hospital gown, propped up against two big pillows. What hair he's got left has been combed. But he looks like a shadow of the man I used to know only a couple of weeks before.

I take a couple of steps, and he opens his eyes.

I open my mouth to say something, but he gives me a frown and a finger on his lips, then points to the door.

I go over and put my ear against it. I can hear footsteps disappearing down the hall.

"Spies all over the place," Delvin whispers when I go back to sit down. He grabs my arm and almost pulls me over on him. "People pussyfooting around day and night."

"Well, there's nobody lurking outside the door at this minute," I says. "You think they got the room wired?"

He shakes himself, and his eyes seem to come into focus.

"What's the matter with you, Jimbo, you think you fell into a moving picture?"

"You just said—"

"I just said there's always somebody creeping around, peeking in to see if you got an eye open so they should give you another pill. There's one bird pops in and out like a Republican at a Democratic fund raiser. But it's the one wants to dope me up I got to watch out for."

"Why would they want to do that?"

His face crumples up, and he looks from side to side like there's somebody sitting in the shadows in the corners of the room.

"It's because of what I know about the gunmen."

"What gunmen?"

"The lurkers in the alleys. The boyos fighting out there in the streets."

Whoops, I think, the old man's gone round the bend with grief.

"What streets?"

"The streets of Dublin, you silly git."

He's acting like Victor McLachlan in that old movie about the Irish revolt. *The Informer,* I think it was called. All of a sudden he's got a brogue you could cut with a knife.

"What do you mean Dublin?" I says.

"Ahh, bejaaasus, the lad's lost his mind. Give me a hand up on these pillows, for God's sake. Make yourself useful."

I don't think Delvin's been in Dublin in his whole life, having come from the countryside of Ireland with his mother and father when he was just a small boy. He surely wasn't there during any of the troubles then or now, though I've heard him tell lies about his dad's running with the IRA back in seventeen with the rest of the professional Irishmen—some born and raised in Chicago—who hang around saloons and firehouses bragging about their connections to the legendary gunmen who fought for Irish freedom and claim to fight for it still.

"Through streets wide and narrow, alive, alive-o," he starts singing.

"You had any of them pills lately?" I asks.

He shivers again, like he did before, and all of sudden he's the old Delvin again, looking at me with the affectionate contempt the old and wise have for the young and foolish.

"How the hell should I know? You think they'd tell me? They slip it into my stew. I didn't like being dragged here, and they know it." He winks one eye. "You got a dram of summat?" he says like an Irish music-hall comic.

"I don't drink, Mr. Delvin. You know that."

"Just my luck to have a bloody temperance for a warden."

"If you didn't want to come, how come you're even here?" I asks, trying to knock him back on the tracks again.

"I wasn't too good after the funeral," he says, very rational again. "A busybody relative of mine decided to take charge."

"I didn't know you had any relatives living."

"This one showed up and identified himself to me as a second or third cousin."

"You never met him before?"

"Of course I met him. When his mother was buried some years ago."

"How did you recognize him years after?"

"Because he rattled off the names of all my grannies and granddas and aunts and all, didn't he?"

"Is he the one committed you?"

"Committed. You saying I fell off my trike?"

"Signed you in, then. Somebody had to take the responsibility."

"If certain friends had been around, they could've taken responsibility and saved me from all this."

He gives me the eye, but I don't say anything.

"Friends are there when you need them," he almost whispers, his eyes weeping like the eyes of an old elephant.

"Well, I know that. That's why I hurried over to see how you was."

"I should hope so. Off living it up in the fleshpots down south while I was suffering probably the second most grievous loss in my life, the death of my sainted wife—"

"God rest her soul."

"—being the first."

"Mary being with me down in New Orleans, I didn't spend much time in the fleshpots," I says. "Tell me more about this cousin of yours."

"Name's Francis Carmody. His mother named him after me, figuring she'd be setting up her bouncing baby boy for a legacy when he was grown and I was ready to die. Hell of a thing to do, naming a boy Francis just for the chance of a legacy. Hardly know him. Why should I leave him my money? On the other hand, he was there in my hour of need, wasn't he?" He gives me this sly, sidelong look. "And blood's thicker than water, ain't it?"

He's telling me he's ready to leave his money and property to them what are kind to him—as it should be—and I ain't one of them. I feel like telling him that I don't give a rat's ass about him—or anybody else—leaving me anything. But he looks so frail and sick lying there it ain't in me to start a fight with him.

So, not knowing what else to say, I just ask him, "How're you feeling?"

"How would you be feeling if you was torn out of your own bed and put down in some institution full of strange smells?" He tries to wipe away some tears that spill over onto his cheeks, but it's like he can't find his face and just waves his hand vaguely around his ear before the effort gets to be too much for him. "Flies are fierce in this place. Dry as hell, and not a drop to drink. 'The boy stood on the burning deck, his feet was full of blisters. He used to wear his father's pants, but now he wears his sister's.'"

He's snapping in and out of real time like a yo-yo. I can't keep up with him.

"If you don't like it, all you got to do is put on your pants and I'll take you out of here," I says, taking out my handkerchief and wiping his cheeks for him.

"You got your car outside?"

"Yes, I do."

"Right at the curb?"

"I left it parked over by Micek Park."

"Ah, now, you see, that's quite a journey."

"It's only two and a half blocks."

He's looking at me sideways like he's not sure I am who I say I am, like I'm somebody out to trick him but he ain't going to let me see he's on to me.

"Well, you see, Jimmy—that's your name?"

I could weep.

"Well, Jimmy, I don't think I could make it that far. Mrs. Banjo's death knocked me to my knees. I'm still as weak as a kitten. A glass of whiskey might put the bones back in my legs," he adds, hopefully.

"You're going to be weaker if you just let yourself lie there in bed. What do you say we get you dressed and I'll run over and bring the car right up to the front step? We can stop over to Dan Blatna's Sold Out Saloon and have a drink."

"Ah, well, maybe tomorrow, Jimmy. Maybe tomorrow when I'm feeling stronger," he says, very pleasant and sly.

The fact that he won't get right up out of bed and come with me, especially when I promise him a drink, tells me how crazy he is and how weak he's feeling.

"I'm really sorry I was out of town when Mrs. Banjo died," I says.

"Ah, don't I know that, sonny?" he says, and it's the old Delvin again, just as normal as Irish soda bread. "I just wanted you to feel bad because I'm feeling so bad. You're about all I've got left, so you're about all I've got to punish when I don't know who else to hit."

I pat his hand, which is about as big a show of affection as ever passed between us, and he turns it over, grabs my fingers, and won't let go.

"She was very fond of you, was Bridget."

"Bridget?"

"Mrs. Banjo."

"Was that her name?"

"Bridget Banjo. Can you believe?"

"It's got a certain ring."

"More like a strum or a pluck," he says, trying to make a joke.

"Well, all right, enough of that. Bridget was very fond of you. Did I tell you that?"

"I never knew."

"She wasn't one to wear her feelings on her sleeve. She showed people how she felt about them in the way she did for them."

Well, I suppose bringing me lemonades and toddies I never drank could be called acts of affection.

"It's a nice lot," he said.

"What?"

"I said the lot she left you is on a nice street."

"The lot she left me?"

"In her will. Ain't you listening to me?"

"I must've missed a beat."

"Right after you got married Bridget says to me, 'Mr. Delvin, wouldn't it be nice if those two young folks could have a proper house of their own one day? Living in a third-floor flat won't be good enough after the babies come.'"

"Babies?"

"So she provided what she could. She'd bought the lot years ago but never built on it after she come to work for me. It's a nice city lot, with utilities already at the property line, not five blocks from where you live."

He's grinning at me like I should be doing back flips.

"Are you having doubts, Jimmy? Are you thinking that I made all this up? Are you thinking that the old man's gone round the bend?"

"No, no," I says.

"All you got to do is give a call to Itzy Dumkowski, Mrs. Banjo's lawyer. He's in the book."

"I wasn't doubting you," I says. "I was just thinking would I want to move away from Polk Street."

"Five blocks away ain't the moon."

"You don't understand," I says, feeling this funny panic, "I don't want to live anywhere but right there on Polk Street with my friends and neighbors."

"Oh, dear, oh, dear," Delvin sighs. "Mrs. Banjo is turning over in her grave at the sight of a man looking her gift horse in the mouth."

"It's not that I don't appreciate the thought."

"Jimmy, you've got to learn to take your opportunities, whatever, whenever, and wherever they may be. Don't throw away Mrs. Banjo's gift until you've talked it over with your dear wife."

"I'll do that," I says.

"Now I think I'll have a nap. You'll come again tomorrow?" he says, finally letting go of my hand.

In the time it takes me to stand up he starts to nod off. I hear him mutter, "That Jimbo. What have I done wrong?" and then he's fast asleep.

I leave and start down the hall.

All of a sudden this little woman comes popping out of another room. She's wearing a flannel nightgown nearly down to the floor, but I can see she's in her bare feet. She's got on an old chenille bathrobe—which has lost most of its little puff-balls—over her nightgown. There's a tatty pink bow in her hair.

"I see you come out of Delvin's room," she says.

"That's right."

"What a grand old man he is."

There's a wild look in her eye, and she clutches my sleeve like she needs me to hold her up while she looks this way and that, half bent over, peering into every corner as we shuffle along.

"What are you looking for, ma'am?" I asks.

"Mice," she says.

"Mice?"

"You know. What to listen with."

"Oh, sure. You got to watch out for them," I says.

"Your name's Flannery, ain't it?" she says.

"Yes, ma'am. How do you know that?"

"Delvin—he's a grand old man, ain't he?—told me all about his right-hand man with the red hair."

"Well, he told you the truth."

"I got something to tell you," she says. Then she screams this little thin scream, and her eyes get big.

I turn my head to look just in time to see a rat go skittering along the baseboard and disappear into a hole. I also hear the sound of Evergreen's heels tapping along the linoleum coming toward us.

"They's everywhere," the old woman says, and she hurries back to her room. "Listening. Listening," she calls back over her shoulder, like it's a secret between her and me.

Evergreen stops alongside me.

"Mrs. Spencer," she says. "Poor old Agnes. Did she have a secret to tell you?"

"I don't know. She said something about listening mice."

"Oh, yes."

"I don't know about mice," I says, "but I just saw a rat as big as a kitten."

"Roof rats. They're all over the neighborhood."

"They don't seem to bother you."

"Oh, they bother me, Mr. Flannery, but exterminators cost a lot of money."

# 5

I go back home with these mixed feelings. Mixed feelings about this gift of a lot that Mrs. Banjo leaves me and mixed feelings about leaving Delvin in the nursing home.

There's something about the whole scene that keeps on haunting me.

That night Mike's over for supper. Mary's mother, Charlotte, and her Aunt Sada are also there, Sada having invited themselves over so she could hear all about our trip to New Orleans. We're having Irish stew and fresh soda bread.

"Potemkin," I says.

"What?" Mike says.

"Huh?" I says.

"You sit there with your face in your plate, a million miles away. All of a sudden you say Potemkin, which I know is the name of some Russian, but I don't know why you'd be mentioning his name at the supper table unless it's somebody in city politics I don't know," Mike says.

"He was a politician, but not in Chicago politics. He was a big favorite of Catherine the Great. The man what dreamed up the idea of building these false-front villages and dressing up a couple of hundred peasants so that when Catherine went on a tour to see how her people was getting along it'd look like everything was

**43**

hunky-dory when all the time behind the scenes they was starving to death and living in poverty you wouldn't believe."

"Your son-in-law, the historian," Aunt Sada says, looking at her sister.

Sada would like me to have ambitions for being more than a sewer inspector. She knows I've had chances to do better, that I maybe could've even took over the department once upon a time before the reform government—which really just replaced the old patronage with their own—got into office.

Even now I got friends with them who'd put in a word to promote me to the spot that, no doubt, Delvin's going to have to give up, if I want to spend my entire savings account of political favors.

So she likes to nudge me every once in a while, but she don't poke me too hard or too often because, on the other hand, she respects me for wanting to stay where I am on the political ladder, her theory being that the farther away a politician gets from the neighborhoods and the people the more harm and the less good he can do.

"Why are you thinking about Russians?" Mary asks.

"Because when I go over to the Larkspur Nursing Home I get a funny feeling."

"It was a Potemkin village?" Sada says.

"That's right. It's got a nice lawn with delphiniums growing up against the porch. And there's wicker rocking chairs on it with nobody sitting in them. Inside there's maybe six old people, all cleaned up in their geriatric chairs, goggling at a big-screen television set. Then you go walking down the hall and things start to get threadbare and seedy."

"I don't know if that means anything," Mary says. "You go backstage at Passavant or any other public facility and I think you'll find the linoleum worn down to the wood and soot piling up on the window sills."

"The first time I go over, there's nobody at the front desk, and somebody's yelling bloody murder, so I go have a look. Two orderlies is tying this old lady, must be ninety, a hundred, to the bed. She's half-naked and cursing a blue streak."

"Aeschrolalia," Mary says. "Compulsive filthy language. It's a psychotic symptom."

"I heard about that before," Mike says. "Years ago there was this old man, Dinty Danaher, lived on our block, used to go down the street in his nightshirt using language would burn the ears off the devil hisself. He was harmless otherwise."

"They're out on the street corners now," Sada chips in. "Nobody to take care of them. Living in cardboard boxes. They curse you as you walk by. Even after you give them what change you've got sometimes."

It looks like everybody in the world but me knows what is this aeschrolalia.

"They may have had to restrain the old lady to keep her from hurting herself, Jimmy," Mary says, putting her hand on mine. "I've had to help tie down a patient more than once myself."

"Also," I says, "I see another orderly threaten this old man walking around with a suit jacket on over his hospital gown. He yells in his face and tells him he don't like him because he's so old he stinks."

"That sounds pretty bad to me," Charlotte says.

Mary leaves go my hand and pays attention to her dinner plate. She's got this look on her face that I notice professionals get when you start criticizing what goes on in their business.

"Don't you think that's pretty bad, Mary?" I says.

"Yes, I do, James. But all you're doing is telling us unrelated incidents." She don't want to go against me in front of everybody but I get the feeling she'd like to tell me I don't know what I'm talking about. That I'm jumping to conclusions, going off half-cocked.

"Unrelated to what?" I asks, not wanting to let it go.

"Unrelated to the situation the orderly may have found himself in."

"You mean he could've had an excuse?"

"No, no. Not an excuse. An explanation. These orderlies in these nursing homes are working for minimum wages. They have no education. They're at the bottom of the social ladder."

"They're doing good work," Charlotte says softly.

"That's right," Mary says. "But there's not much sustenance in being called an angel of mercy nowadays, Ma. Oh, we make a fuss over a couple of Sister Theresas here and there. That's to make us feel good. But the truth is everybody wants somebody else to play Jesus Christ on our behalf. Do the dirty work. Tend the dying. We don't want to do for our own anymore. Not many of us."

"That almost sounds like a sermon, Mary," I says mildly.

"Don't mind me. I'm just trying to tell you, James, that the orderly may have been at the end of a fourteen-hour shift. He may have had troubles of his own. The old man might've been making him a lot of extra trouble."

"That's no excuse."

"I said it was an explanation. I can understand how it might've been. I've been at the end of my own rope enough times."

"But you never yelled in anybody's face."

This rueful little smile quirks the corner of her mouth.

"I've come very close," she says. "Very close, indeed."

"If they were violating patient rights as a matter of policy, Jimmy," Charlotte says in this reasonable, soft way she has, "why would they have done so in front of a stranger being shown around?"

"I wasn't being shown around. The first time I went to see Delvin I wasn't supposed to be there. They'd already told me visiting hours didn't start until two o'clock, and it was just after ten."

"Every hospital and nursing home tries to get the housekeeping and essential patient care done in the morning," Mary says, her mouth a little tight because I'm still going on about things she figures I don't know all that much about. "I don't think you should have ignored their rules."

"I give them that, Mary," I says. "I understand they got a time do what they got to do. I broke the rules because I was worried about not being at the funeral when Delvin needed me. So I go to his room without anybody seeing me, and it's filthy. It stinks. I can tell he's wet hisself or worse, and nobody's come around to do anything about it. On top of it all, he's so drugged out he don't even know it when I sit there for ten minutes holding his hand."

"Oh, Jimmy," Mary says, her eyes all soft and loving, reaching out to put her hand over mine again, "there could be a hundred and one explanations. His own room getting cleaned. A sudden burst of admissions. A day unusually short-staffed, worse than usual."

"But when I go back at the regular time—"

"Almost four hours later?" Mary says.

"—he's in a room with a picture on the wall and flowers on the table, lying in a clean bed in a clean gown with his hair combed."

"Well, there you are," she says, like I'd just made her case for her.

Looking at it from her angle, I can see I look like somebody looking for trouble where there ain't no trouble.

"Well, I said it was only a feeling," I says, unable to make a better argument for my uneasiness than the one I already made.

"What city office is responsible for the administration of nursing homes and private nursing hospitals?" Charlotte asks, giving me a chance to save a little face.

"Department of Aging and Disability?" Mike says, like he's only making a suggestion.

"Department of Health?" Sada says.

"Community Services?" Charlotte chips in.

"Senior Citizens Services?" Mary says.

"Maybe I should make a couple of calls," I says, in this lame way, ready to drop it.

But Mike sees a chance for a little comment. "Don't go stepping on any toes," he warns me.

"What are you telling me that for?"

"I'm just saying don't start rattling any cages or rocking any boats before you got a better idea what's what."

"How's that? You telling me to walk on eggs?" I says, getting a little warm under the collar.

"I'm telling you not to rock the boat. Delvin's on his back, and you can bet yourself a dollar not only won't he be the sewer boss much longer, but Ray Carrigan, as the head of the party organization, and Wally Dunleavy, as the Superintendent of Streets and Sanitation, will be looking to name a new committeeman for the Twenty-seventh and a new super for the sewers."

They're all looking at me. Without them saying anything, I know what they're thinking. I blew my chance to take over as alderman in the Twenty-seventh when Delvin wanted to throw me his coat and Janet Canarias, the lipstick lesbian, ran independent and won.

Sometimes the alderman is also the committeeman, but sometimes not. So even with Canarias representing the Twenty-seventh in the council, this is a chance—maybe the last chance I'll get—to be the Democratic Party boss of the ward. Also I might still have a shot at the top job in the sewers, if I want to bankrupt myself like I already said.

Like it, don't like it, I'm being faced with big choices that could change our lives, Mary and me. It's just that I got this awful feeling they could be changes for the worse, not the better.

"Well, anyway, when I go back after lunch," I says, "they got Delvin all cleaned up and in a new room. He acts a little goofy, but I figure that's from whatever they was giving him to calm him down and ease his grief. He'd like go in and out, saying screwy things one minute and being perfectly okay the next. While he's acting okay this one time he tells me Mrs. Banjo left me a vacant lot."

I drop that like it's just an extra piece of news of no importance.

"She what?" Mike says.

"It looks like Mrs. Banjo didn't have nobody else to leave it to, so she left it to me."

"You sure Delvin wasn't hallucinating?"

"He gives me the name of Mrs. Banjo's lawyer. Itzy Dumkowski. I give him a call, and he tells me, sure enough, Mrs. Banjo left me this piece of property over by Horan Park."

Charlotte and Sada are looking at Mary, and I can tell that whenever they've been talking about Mary and me and what kind of a future Mary can look forward to, having a house and a family comes up more than just every once in a while.

"A house of your own, Mary," Charlotte says.

And from the way Mary's eyes are shining I know there's no getting out of this one. There's going to be some changes made, whether I like it or not.

"When I left Delvin the second time, I saw a rat," I says.

"Roof rats," Mary says. "Exterminating them is a budget item at Passavant."

# 6

The next day I got work to do, including all the paperwork I was going to catch up on the day before but didn't.

A lot of people think that just because I work for the city I sit around all day doing nothing and just stop in at City Hall every two weeks to collect my pay. But I got plenty to do, and if you ever want to know what it takes to keep the crap a few million people produce every day moving through the guts of the city, come on down to the ward office on West Madison and I'll give you the two-dollar tour.

When lunchtime rolls around I decide to go over to Dan Blatna's Sold Out Saloon, which is way over in the Thirty-second. I go there a lot because my old man and me get into the habit once upon a time when we can't agree on giving our business to a restaurant in the Fourteenth, where he's a precinct captain, or in the Twenty-seventh, where I'm a precinct captain. So we compromise on the Sold Out Saloon, which also happens to make the best kielbasa and cabbage in the city.

Blatna's is also the latest hangout for some of the reporters and columnists from the *Tribune* and the *Sun-Times,* who're like a bunch of gypsies going from restaurant to restaurant and bar to bar until they wear out their welcome in one place and got to go looking for another.

Just like I figure, Joe Medill, who's got a column in the *Trib,* and

Jackie Boyle, who's got a column in the *Times,* are sitting in a booth drinking beer and not talking to each other.

They've been carrying on this feud for fifteen years. Like a lot of husbands and wives, they stick around together to make sure one don't stab the other in the back. They want to see where the other one's hands is at all times. Sometimes they quarrel, and sometimes they sulk.

Today they're sulking.

When I walk over, Boyle says, "How's it floating, Jimmy?"

When I don't crack a smile he adds, "A little sanitation humor there, Jimmy."

"Think that's humorous, do you?" Medill says, speaking up in a voice that sounds like a rusty faucet. "Making fun of a man's profession."

"Jimmy and me is old friends," Boyle says. "You wouldn't know about how old friends show their affection with such remarks."

"Does that mean I can sit down, old friend?" I says.

"Grab a pee-u," Boyle says.

"A little combination church and sewer humor there?" Medill says, pulling a sour face.

I sit down next to Boyle, who gives me the invitation, even though I know this could irritate Medill. On the other hand, if I sit down next to Medill, Boyle could get his nose out of joint. If you know these two, you got to be very careful how and why you do what, and even then you'll probably make one of them mad at you.

"Congratulations, Jimmy," Medill says, "I hear you're going to start building your own home."

"How in the hell do you know that?" I asks.

Medill grins and pulls down the lid on one eye like he's a man who knows all, sees all.

"Your old man left not five minutes ago," Boyle says. "Had himself a plate of sausage and told us all about Delvin and old Mrs. Banjo and your legacy."

"Then you know Delvin's over to this place called the Larkspur Nursing Home."

"That news is all over town. Are you finally going to accept the mantle, Jimmy?" Medill asks.

"Are you going to be the new warlord of the Twenty-seventh?" Boyle adds.

"It ain't been offered lately."

"I don't know if it's worth having anymore, Jimmy," Boyle says. "Unless you decide to run for alderman."

"Janet Canarias has the job, and I got no complaints with the way she's doing it."

"If you want to go up the ladder, Jimmy, you got to put a foot on all the rungs. The machine ain't strong enough for committee-man to mean much right this minute. You got to run for office, too."

"You're going to be a home owner, Jimmy," Medill chimes in. "That means you got extra opportunities and extra obligations."

"About this Larkspur operation," I says.

"What about it?" Boyle says.

"You hear any sour notes, smell any stinks?"

"The nursing homes in Chicago have been in trouble since sixty-nine, when the Illinois State Legislature, the State Depart-ment of Health, and the governor decided on policy changes that released a flood of old people, a lot of them mentally incompetent, out of the state mental hospitals," Boyle says.

"They flooded the nursing care homes and shelters," Medill says, adding his two bits.

"Economics," Boyle goes on. "It costs a grand a month to keep a patient in a state hospital and only three hundred in the nursing homes."

"You wouldn't think they could make a profit at them prices, would you?" Medill says.

"But the director of the State Psychiatric Association testified at subcommittee hearings that he was offered bribes of one hundred bucks a head to place this or that mental patient in this or that nursing home," Boyle says.

"Larkspur in on that?" I asks.

"It never came to charges, but they were named."

"It never came to charges, because the hearings were just investigatory and advisory proceedings," Medill elaborates.

"By nineteen seventy-two they were all forgotten. Nursing

homes in Uptown were flooded with these old people. New homes sprang up like mushrooms overnight and spread out all over the city. There were bucks to be made, and the state was in on it, too."

"How's that?"

"It was doing what it could to balance its own budget. Not only was it saving the grand a month per head by moving them out of state hospitals, but the cost to the state to keep them in nursing care facilities was reduced by the fed welfare program passed that year to the tune of an extra hundred and fifty-seven bucks per head," Boyle says. "You want a beer?"

"Nothing for me," I says.

"You want a beer, Joe?"

"Why not?" Medill says.

Boyle catches the eye of a passing waiter and holds up two fingers, then points to his stein.

"The hundred and fifty-seven bucks was supposed to be paid to the individual, not to nursing homes," Medill says, "but it ends up in the state's pocket to offset the three hundred a month it had to pay for keeping the indigent in the nursing homes."

"And the welfare recipients end up with twenty-five bucks a month spending money."

"Which they don't always get either."

"Is this getting too complicated for you, Jimmy?" Boyle asks, grinning in this superior way he's got.

"Maybe I don't understand all the words," I says, "but I sure recognize the tune."

"Everybody's making a nickel, a dime, except that everybody's also making a poor mouth," Boyle says.

"Everybody's losing money. So they say." Medill picks it up. "Except whenever the nursing homes are ordered to prove their case by opening up their books they refuse, resist, and generally duck the offer."

"Why ain't you writing about this?" I says.

"We are. We did. In sixty-nine we made a case against shifting this huge hospital population out of state mental facilities into homes that weren't equipped to handle it. In seventy-two we wrote it up when Congress passed a statute making offering or receiving a kickback a crime worth a year and ten large if convicted. In seventy-four we told the public the statute was hardly enforceable. In seventy-six Skinner, the U.S. Attorney for the northern district of Illinois, got some convictions, but then the crooks got a little smarter and buried the rest of the indictments in a blizzard of sales, transfers, and paperwork."

"So there's plenty more. We even got a citizens' watchdog committee with ombudsmen running all over the city, sticking their noses in, writing up reports. Does the public pay attention? Do you pay attention, Jimmy?" Medill asks as the waiter delivers the two beers.

"Of course you don't," he goes on, Boyle being too busy sucking the head off his stein. "You got other fish to fry. That's understandable. There's too many fires and not enough firemen. Too many holes in the dike and not enough fingers."

Boyle opens his mouth and releases some gas. He don't say excuse me. Only ladies say excuse me at the Sold Out.

"So now you're interested because your old Chinaman's in one of these smelly warehouses," he says.

"Nothing wrong with that, is there?" I says. "Wanting to take care of your own."

"No, but it's funny if you look at it one way," Medill says.

"What way is that?"

"Well, when these new corporations start looking for venture capital to get in on the nursing home action, who do you think was right there with their investment money in their hot little paws?"

"The politicians, Jimmy, the politicians," Boyle says.

"And guess who was some of the first in line?"

Now it's coming, the punch line they been waiting to deliver. The reason why they started tossing information my way turn and turn about like a team of jugglers. The reason they was having so much fun that they even forgot to be mad at each other.

"The old warlord, Chips Delvin," Boyle says, pulling the pin.

"And his old friend, the head of Streets and Sanitation, Wally Dunleavy," Medill says, catching it on the fly.

"And that wise old white-on-white sage in the black suit, Ray Carrigan, chairman of the Cook County Democratic Party Organization," Boyle says.

"And Perkanola, the Chief of Medicine down at the Health Department."

"And Hackman, the medical examiner."

"A little conflict of interest there, you think, Jimmy?"

"Or do you think they all thought they were investing in a vacation condominium?" Medill says with a smile, finishing off the routine.

# 7

I go downtown to see Wally Dunleavy, the chief of Streets and
Sanitation. He's probably the oldest city employee in town except
for maybe Kippy Kerner, who supervises the guy what adjusts the
valves on the furnaces in City Hall, and Billy Swinarski who sits at
a desk in the lobby in front of the city treasurer's office telling
people where is the city treasurer's office.

If there's a dead-end alley in the city Dunleavy don't know
about, somebody built it last night without a permit. If there's a
shylock or gonif doing business without Dunleavy knowing
everything about him or her, they was just born.

He's got this trick. The minute you walk into the front office,
one of his people recognizes you, or asks your name if you're a
first-timer. The word goes to somebody else, who starts looking
you up in the files. If you been there before, that takes maybe a
minute. If you're a new face, it takes a little longer, because they
maybe got to make a couple telephone calls or look you up in the
voters' roll or the landowners' register or here and there. Then
they stall you a little bit, asking you how you like the weather, until
they know all there is to know about you and old Dunleavy's been
primed.

I been in so many times my file's practically on the corner of
Dunleavy's desk. The whole thing is worked so that when you
walk in he can give you the glad hand like he's been thinking about

nothing but you all day and can't believe his good luck you should walk through his door. Like you're his favorite person and he spends half his day keeping up on what's happening in your life. An old politician's trick. Men have become president with that trick.

So when I walk through the door to his office, which is like at the center of a maze, there's Dunleavy huddled over his maps and plats, peering up at me over the tops of his glasses and grinning at me like I'm his long-lost nephew.

"Jimmy Flannery, ain't it?"

"How are you, Mr. Dunleavy?"

"The years are nibbling away at my memory. How's your father, Mike?" he says, proving that his memory's pretty good after all.

"Couldn't be better."

"I wish we could say the same about old Delvin," he says, putting down his red pencil and leaning back in his chair with a sad look on his face that barely covers up his joy at being hale and hearty when a man a year or two younger than him is lying on his back in a nursing home.

It's not that he's actually happy for somebody else's misfortune, it's just that he just can't help feeling good because somebody else is feeling bad when he's feeling good.

"Sorry to hear about Mrs. Banjo," he goes on. "Great friend of yours, was she?"

"To tell you the truth, Mr. Dunleavy, I never knew we was good friends until after she passed away."

"God rest her soul. So her gift to you came as a great surprise, did it?"

I figure the whole town knows Mrs. Banjo left me a piece of property by now.

"Is it about the lot you've come to see me?" he goes on.

"I'm thinking about building, and I was wondering if there's anything I should know about it before I start."

He knows and I know he knows that I'm asking for a favor here, a little word from him in the right places down at the Water Management Board or the Building Department, anything that'll smooth the way and maybe save me a couple of dollars without taking the bread out of anybody's mouth.

"You mean anything like does the land sit on top of a spot of archeological significance, like some old Indian cemetery or a battlefield of the Civil War?" he says, arching his eyebrows, reminding me of the time, not very long ago, when I salted the graveyard behind St. Pat's over on the Southeast Side with Indian artifacts because an oil company was going to disinter some distant relatives of Delvin's, moving them elsewhere so a gas station could be erected on the spot.

"Well, yes, something like that, or anything else," I says, giving him a little grin, meaning that we were both sharing the joke.

"Oh, I think we can see your house goes up with a minimum of bother," he says. "Now, tell me, have you been to see old Delvin?"

"I have."

"I've been meaning to go myself, though I've got to admit walking into a place like that with all them old bones sitting around in their skins doing nothing gives me the willies. However did he land up there?"

"Francis Carmody persuaded him. You ever hear tell of this Carmody?"

"I've heard the name."

"What's his connection to Delvin?"

"He's a cousin by marriage twice removed. Something like that. I never can figure out them family trees."

"How come I never heard of him before?"

"Maybe because Delvin don't mention him to you before."

"How come he don't mention him?"

"How the hell am I supposed to know, Jimmy? Maybe because he don't think it's any of your business."

"Come on, Mr. Dunleavy, why would he hide a relative from me?"

"I ain't saying he hid him. I'm saying he never mentioned him. We know each other how long? Maybe twenty years? You think I ever told you about every nephew, niece, and cousin I got?"

"I know you maybe twelve, thirteen years, Mr. Dunleavy, but Delvin's been my Chinaman for twenty, and I think we talk a lot more to each other than you and me ever done."

He rears back in his chair and looks me over. "I never see a guy like you, Flannery. You see a piece of mouse shit and you ask

'Where's the elephant?' So Chips never mentions this cousin. So what? Maybe it's because he likes to play the part of the last Delvin in the family. So when he dies that's the end of the line, and 'ain't that sad?' Maybe he don't mention this Carmody because he don't ever *think* about this Carmody."

"The man's mother named Carmody after Chips."

"She named a baby Chips?"

"No, she named him Francis."

"So maybe Chips suspects this woman names her kid after him because she thinks it'll pay off when he passes on without having any kids of his own. And maybe Delvin don't like the presumption. She didn't know him very well, that's for sure, or she'd've known he hates the name Francis. What's this all by way of, Jimmy?"

"Carmody appears at the funeral out of the blue and takes over. He checks Delvin into a rest home called the Larkspur."

I don't see a flicker. Maybe Boyle and Medill ain't got their facts straight. Maybe they're just passing on gossip. Maybe Dunleavy ain't got any money into this nursing home operation.

"It ain't the best-run hotel in the world," I says. "You heard of this place?"

He purses his lips.

"It's called the Larkspur," I go on, "and it's right by Micek Park," I tell him.

He frowns a little bit.

"Something bothering you, Mr. Dunleavy? You heard about this nursing home?"

"The name sounds familiar, but I can't seem to place it."

"Maybe you heard about the conditions there. They're pretty bad, I think."

"Can't place it."

"Ain't it in your files?"

"Sure, it'll be in there. I'll have it looked up."

"Maybe if you looked it up under investments," I says.

"Run that train through the station one more time, will you?" he says, his jaw tightening up some.

I know I should let it drop, but something won't let me. "You might have a financial interest in the Larkspur," I says.

He don't like my tone of voice, but he just looks at me sideways a little.

"Something bothering you, Jimmy? You got a wild hair?"

"Nothing like that, Mr. Dunleavy. I'm just asking do you know the kind of place you've got your money invested in."

"Are you upbraiding me, Jimbo? Is there something about where my financial managers put my money that you disapprove of?"

He's trying to make it look like he's got people investing his money for him without his knowledge, but I know and he knows I know that there ain't a penny passes through his hands that he ain't put an address on.

"Nowadays things are so complicated a man can't just stick his money in the bank and draw his two or three percent," he says. "We got futures. We got debentures. We got options and options on options. We got . . . well, what the hell, you know how it is. Nothing's simple and straightforward anymore when it comes to money. You got to hire somebody to take care of it."

I'm ready to say that nothing about money was ever very simple and straightforward, it was people who used to be simple and straightforward and maybe weren't anymore. I was going to say he'd rather cut his wrists than pay anybody to take care of his money. But his eyes are a little icy, and I know I better not pester the animals too much.

"Who told you I had any money invested in this nursing home?" he asks.

"It's around."

"That's all you can say?"

"There ain't any more."

He's picking up his red pencil, telling me he's got no more time for me. "Don't go looking for any niggers in the woodpile, Flannery," he says.

"I'll just tell Mr. Delvin you'll be by to see him and have a look around," I says, getting to my feet.

"If things is so bad over there," Dunleavy says, "what the hell you leaving him there for?"

"Well, I'm looking into ways to get him out," I says.

"Yes, you do that. You look into it and I'll look into it, and we'll see what's what."

He goes back to the map he's working on.

"All anybody's doing is trying to put a little aside for their old age," he says, like he's talking to himself.

"What did you say, Mr. Dunleavy?"

"I says, you look into it and I'll look into it, and we'll do what we can do without making the six o'clock news. Right?"

"Yes, sir."

# 8

Mike's over for supper, which ain't unusual. Tonight he brings three dozen ears of first-crop sweet corn. Mary boils up the corn. We each got a stick of butter to ourselves to roll the ears in. There's also some apple pie if anybody wants it.

"There's enough cholesterol in all this butter to stun our hearts," Mary says, working her way through her dozen ears of corn.

"It only happens once a year, at the beginning of corn season," Mike says, "so I ain't going to feel too guilty. I'll run a couple extra miles. Speaking of which, when are you going to buy yourself a pair of Nikes or Reeboks and come run a few with me, Jim?"

"I got to rework my schedule, see how I can fit it in."

"No time like the present. Right after supper put on your old tennis shoes, and we'll go down to Grant Park and do some laps."

"Not on a full stomach I'm not going to do laps. You could die from it. Ain't that right, Mary?"

"It probably wouldn't do you any good, seeing the condition you're in."

Mike's pleased that she agrees with him that I'm not in such great shape.

"What's the matter with my condition? I been walking miles every day for years. I don't know that buying a track suit and some

fancy sneakers and running around a hard track hurting my ankles and knees is going to get me in better shape."

"You used to walk miles every day when you was walking the sewers, but you ain't been doing that—except for that little punishment tour old Delvin gave you—in longer than I can remember," Mike says.

I'm ready to start an argument when there's a knock on the front door.

"That would be the lawyer," Mike says.

"What lawyer?"

"The lawyer what handled Mrs. Banjo's will. I forgot to tell you. He called when you two was out and told me he'd be glad to come over here to deliver the deed to that vacant lot and get you to sign a paper."

Mary's gone to the door and comes back with Itzy Dumkowski. He's a fat character wearing about twelve yards of blue serge suit, a shirt so white it could burn your eyes, and a red satin tie. He looks like a flag walking around. He smiles around his teeth on all four sides and sticks out his hand, first to me and then to my old man, who apologizes for any grease he could have on his hand.

"Sweet corn," Dumkowski says.

"There's a few ears left," Mary says. "Would you like to have them?"

"I wouldn't want to deprive anyone," he says, sitting down and reaching for a couple of paper napkins. He puts a bulging, well-worn briefcase on the floor by his shoe with one hand while he's tucking in the corner of a napkin with the other. When he spreads it out it only covers part of his shirt, so he takes the second and tucks it in between a couple of buttons on his shirt so the rest of him'll be safe.

"I always say, 'Go into the house of the common working man'—no offense intended—'and you'll get hospitality you'll never get in the homes of the aristocratic rich.' "

He finishes off the four ears Mary had left over just about the time Mike and me finish the rest of ours.

Mary brings over the pie and cuts it into eight pieces.

Mike pours out the coffee.

Dumkowski inhales his piece of pie and looks round eyes until Mary asks him would he like another.

He's having his third piece of pie and second cup of coffee while the rest of us are just watching him.

I never see a man enjoy his food so much. Not even my old man when Mary makes stew and Irish soda bread. He's having such a good time that we all just sit there grinning at him.

Tonight there ain't going to be no pie for Mike and me while we're watching the ten o'clock news. Dumkowski finishes it all but refuses a fourth cup of coffee and says, "It's time to get down to business."

Reaching over sideways and sliding down in the chair a little, he manages to get his hand on the briefcase and put it on his lap. Or on his knees, really, because he ain't got much of a lap.

"I can't tell you what a pleasure this part of my profession is," he says. "Passing on the gifts of the dear departed to surviving friends and loved ones makes it all worthwhile."

I don't ask him what's so hard about the rest of what he does.

He hands over the deed to the property and a paper I sign proving that he's executed his duty to the satisfaction of the trustee, who happens to be Delvin.

"You know Mr. Delvin a long time?" I asks.

"Casually. Only casually. I was Mrs. Banjo's attorney for twenty years, but I never had reason to see much of her employer. I had an introduction. Always do that. Get an introduction from one client hoping to get another. Good business practice," he says while he's handing a calling card to each one of us. "But Mr. Delvin had plenty of long-standing legal counsel of his own. I drew up Mrs. Banjo's will, though, and since Mr. Delvin was named her trustee I had reason to confer with him."

"You've seen him, then?" I says.

"I spoke to him at the wake."

"How did he seem to you?"

"Confused. Almost prostrate with grief. It hits the old ones very hard, you know. Part of it's the survival syndrome. They're still alive when people younger than them are dying, and that makes for a burden of guilt. Time of tragedy is a dangerous time even putting that aside. When my own father died, his brother dropped dead at the funeral, my mother went down with a flu that lasted two weeks—thought it'd turn into pneumonia and we'd lose her—and my brother had a heart attack. Mild, but still, there you go, stress and grief. Takes a terrible toll. I had an attack of gall bladder myself. Everybody suffers."

"He wasn't too confused to know what you was talking about?" I says, managing to sneak the question in edgeways. I can see that Dumkowski's the sort of man, you ask him a three-second question, he gives you a five-minute answer.

"I'm not a medical man, you understand. Still and all, in my profession . . ." I hardly know I'm doing it, but I raise my hand and hold it with the palm looking at him, like I'm a traffic cop, and he stops rattling on and says, "His responses were slow but unimpaired. Has he suggested to you that I'm not handling this matter efficiently or correctly?"

"Nothing like that. Oh, no. I was just wondering, if his head was working all right, why he let hisself be put into a nursing home." I raise my hand. It works again. I get short answers whenever I do it.

"That would have been at his cousin's suggestion," he says.

"Carmody?"

"That's right. You know him, I'm sure."

"I didn't even know that Mr. Delvin had any living relatives until just the other day."

"Well, fortunately for him, he seems to have at least one. Mr. Carmody appeared to be a tower of strength at the wake. The kind of man prepared to take responsibility during a time when Mr. Delvin, fragile with grief, would need someone to see after his affairs. I should imagine that a man of his wealth would have considerable holdings and investments needing constant review."

I glance at Mike. I can see that it never occurs to him, just like it never occurs to me, that Delvin probably has got a bundle he's collected over the years in city government so big that he couldn't stuff it in a sock or under the mattress.

"But with Carmody taking over like you say, Delvin still makes the decisions as trustee for Mrs. Banjo?" I says.

"There wasn't much to be decided. Her estate is very modest. There aren't even any tax consequences to consider. The vacant lot she left to you, a few bequests of cash to friends—none greater than a thousand dollars—her photographs, china and silver, already in his house, to Mr. Delvin, and some charitable gifts here and there. The whole lot no more than eighty thousand dollars. Very modest nowadays. Especially when you consider the lot makes up more than half of it."

"Is a vacant lot in this part of town worth forty, fifty thousand dollars?" I says, really surprised.

"Give or take five thousand. Would you be thinking of selling it?"

"We don't know what we intend to do," Mary says. "Not right this minute. Mrs. Banjo's gift came as quite a surprise."

"Well, if ever you want to sell, please contact me. Real-estate law is one of my specialties."

"We'll do that, Mr. Dumkowski," I says. "You talk to Delvin only that once?"

"Well, no. I talked to him two times since. Once on the telephone a few hours after he was settled into the nursing home the first day, and once late this afternoon."

"How did he sound?"

"Drowsy. In fact, we only spoke for a moment, and then Mr. Carmody got on the phone and answered the few questions I wanted to put to Mr. Delvin."

"Would you like another cup of coffee?" Mary asks.

"I've had a sufficiency, thank you," he says, patting his stomach with both hands. After that he gets up and leaves.

# 9

The next day I go down to the building department, which in Chicago is called the Department of Inspectional Services—don't ask me why—over on LaSalle.

Inspectional Services includes Building Complaints and Information, Building Permits, the Compliance Board, Bureau of Licensing Registration and Permits, the Board of Examiners for Mason Contractors, Plumbers, and Stationary Engineers and the Commissioner's Office.

I know people in practically every department of the city and got good relationships with every one of them. Except I ain't got such grand relationships with anybody in the commissioner's office or in Building Complaints and Information because I've had to go to both places and raise hell when some of my neighbors come to me with complaints about the flats they got to live in.

Also, I don't know anybody in Permits, because I never had the occasion, and they change clerks like a jockey changes silks.

I step up to the counter—which is marked and scarred by fifty years of doodles put there while contractors and common people like me waited for somebody to admit they was alive—with the deed to the vacant lot in my hand.

A kid, maybe eighteen, maybe nineteen, is sitting there reading a comic book. I clear my throat three times before he looks up and asks me what I want.

"I want to build a house."

"You got funny papers?"

"Funny papers?"

"Plans."

"I'm just trying to find out what I got to do before I start looking at plans."

"So you ain't got a contractor either?"

"I'm trying to take the first step is what I'm trying to do. Are you the man can help me?"

He likes that, me calling him a man. He puts down the comic book, hops off the stool and comes over to lean on the counter.

"I got a deed to the land," I says.

"That's all right. It ain't up to me to check if the deed's good, it ain't good."

"You mean anybody can walk in, say they want to build a house on a vacant lot, and you don't care if they can prove they own it?"

He looks at me like he pities my ignorance.

"Don't worry, somebody'll check. You got the deed recorded? Well, it's a matter of the public record, ain't it?"

I give him a little grin like I'm saying how dopey can I get, having learned a long time ago that a little stupid can go a long way with certain people who want to feel that their jobs are more important than they really are. "I never thought."

"So, there, that's one thing you don't have to worry about. What you got to do, number one, is get the lot surveyed so you're sure about the boundaries."

"Wasn't it surveyed when the subdivision went through?"

"Sure, and it was surveyed the first time it was sold and every time it was sold or transferred after that."

"How come is that? Do they think the land moved a foot one way or the other?"

He wiggles his eyebrows. "Hey, whattaya think? Surveyors got to make a living. Number two is you get some drawings made up." He whips out a piece of paper from under the counter. "This'll tell you how much coverage you're allowed on the property. How much square footage can be contained in the building envelope. What kind of setbacks you need front and back and on the sides. How much of the lot can be covered by impermeable surfaces, like driveways and permanent walkways." He stares into my eyes for a minute, then says, "You better get yourself a builder."

So after I pay two hundred and fifty bucks to get things rolling, I go home and call up my old man.

"Who do you know what can build me a house?" I says.

"You know what kind of house you want?" he asks.

"I figure two floors in that neighborhood. Two bedrooms and a bath and half. Nice living room."

"Fireplace?"

"That would be nice."

"Step-down?"

"Step-down what?"

"Step-down into the living room. It's the thing nowadays."

"Somebody could trip and break their neck stepping up, stepping down."

"Well, that would be bad, but your homeowner's would cover it."

"Cover what?"

"Any injuries visitors might sustain coming on your property. From the gate and up the walk, on the front stoop and inside the house."

"What do I need that for? I ain't got no homeowner's insurance where I'm living."

"You ain't got a house they could take away from you. When you're ready for a builder, we'll find you a builder. Talk it over with Mary, what kind of house you want."

"I'll do that."

So that night after supper Mary and me walk over to Horan Park, which is only about five blocks away from where we live, like Delvin says. But I know about five blocks in the city.

Four square blocks, from where the corners meet, is a neighborhood. Another block in every direction is a walk to the tavern or the grocery store or the shoemaker. Any more than that's a visit to a sick relative or a girlfriend when you're a young man. Five blocks when you're older and settled is practically across town. You think you're going to visit your friends in the old neighborhood often, but you don't.

If we move, I'd be seeing my old neighbors more than most

people because I'm always running around doing this and that, but even then I know that I won't be seeing them every day. That's what makes neighbors, seeing them every day. Maybe not even visiting each other's houses or having a meal together. Just seeing them to say hello or even wave to every day.

But it's a nice night and a nice walk over to the pig park, and it don't hurt to talk about it. We sit on a bench across the street and look at the vacant lot sitting between two old houses, which the people living in them obviously care about.

"Two bedrooms and a bath and a half?" I says.

"Three bedrooms, two and half if we can afford it," Mary says.

I understand why she's thinking three bedrooms. For kids. If they're both girls or both boys, okay, two bedrooms for the family's plenty. But if one's a boy and one's a girl, there you go. You got to have a bedroom for each kid. And suppose there's more than two kids. Well, there you got no immediate problem. Girl or boy you can double it up. But say you got four—three of one and one of the other.

Here I am thinking about a house and kids, and it shakes me again that I got to do a little better for myself and for Mary and for the kids we ain't even got yet. I can't be a sewer inspector all my life. I got to reach for bigger and better things.

And that, don't ask me why, gives me the blues.

Mary's like a cat, she senses when things ain't right with me. She won't let me brood about anything but jumps right on it.

"Something bothering you, Jimmy?" she says.

"No, no," I says, doing a quick cover-up, "I was just thinking about what I got to do tomorrow. For one thing, I got to go see how Delvin's doing."

Mary's not dumb. She knows I don't want to talk about building a house anymore. She knows enough to let me cut myself a little slack. So we just sit there holding hands, and after a while we start necking like a couple of teenagers. Only I don't think the kids call it necking anymore.

# 10

The next day is one of those days. I get an emergency call from the ward office at six o'clock in the morning. There's a major toxic spill from some factory into the line feeding the water filtration plant over to Rainbow Park, and all the inspectors and supervisors get called in to put their shoulders to the wheel.

I even got to put on a respirator and a tank and go down into the sewers to see how far the poison has spread downstream.

I can't find five minutes for myself.

By the time I get home I'm worn out and filthy. All I want to do is soak in the tub and maybe sleep there until morning. But Mary comes in and helps dry me off.

"Your father's coming over with that builder friend of his," she reminds me.

When Mike arrives with Stavros Bikas, a Greek with skin like leather and blue eyes buried in a mess of laugh lines, Mary and me've had our supper and I'm sitting at the kitchen table in my underwear and a bathrobe.

I shake hands with Bikas when my old man introduces us, and we look each other over.

"Excuse me. I'll go in and put on my pants," I says.

"What do you need with your pants?" Bikas asks. "You're comfortable without your pants at the end of a long day's work, it's better you sit around in your bathrobe. What a man wants to do in his own home, everybody should respect, ain't that right?"

We all agree on that.

Mary offers him something to drink.

"What are you having?" he says.

"We've got a little wine and some beer, but we're having coffee."

"Coffee's fine."

"We're having some canned peaches and condensed cream for dessert," I says.

"That'll hit the spot," he says, and he sits down like we've known each other for years. He lays this thick loose-leaf book down on the table.

It's a warm night, so he asks Mary very politely if he can take off his jacket. He's wearing an old-fashioned undershirt without sleeves on underneath. He's got the coloring of a man who's worked outside in the weather all his life. His face, his neck, and his arms halfway up, where he rolls his sleeves, are like brown leather. The rest of him is white as a bone.

The veins stand out on his arms and hands like rope. You can see he's worked hard all his life and he ain't about to slow down.

"Stavros is crowding eighty, would you believe it?" Mike says. "When a job's short-handed he still swings a hammer or lays some brick."

"When I'm sixty-eight," Bikas says, grinning from ear to ear, "I'm working a job over to Evanston. I'm laying brick. The job steward from the union comes over to me. He says, 'Mr. Bikas, you got to slow down.' I says, 'Why for I got to slow down?' He says, 'You layin' too many bricks. You makin' the other men look bad.' I says, 'The other men are thirty, maybe even forty. How come they can't keep up?' 'Well, Mr. Bikas,' he says, 'maybe they could keep up if they wanted to push themselves. But the union only asks bricklayers to lay four hundred bricks a day. You're laying almost eight. So you got to slow down.' 'Well,' I says, 'when I learned my business I was told you give a man an honest day's work for an honest day's pay.' That's what I says."

Mike is beaming at Bikas like he invented him.

"Now I'm a contractor. My crews give me an honest day's work for an honest day's pay," he goes on. "Don't you worry." He opens up the big book. It's filled with page after page of pictures, some a little out of focus, of all kinds of houses.

"Take a look. Pick out a house you like."

I can see Mary's getting excited. The idea of having a house of her own is suddenly real to her. Before, all we was doing was dreaming out loud. Now, here's this little old Greek, tough as an olive tree, ready to turn her dreams and our conversations into sticks and stones.

Bikas and my old man lean back and drink coffee while Mary and me turn over the pages. All of a sudden she puts her finger on a photo of a two-story house with a porch, a couple of bay windows, and what they call dormers in the roof upstairs.

Bikas takes a look.

"That's a nice house. I work on that house thirty years ago. So that's what you want your house to look like? Okay. But first let me tell you that's a big house. It don't look so big in the picture, but it's a big house. I'll make you a house looks like that only smaller. But first of all you better think about it. You don't need a porch. Nobody builds a porch anymore because nobody sits out on a porch anymore. Not in a neighborhood like the one you're going to be building in. People still hang around on the porch or the stoop in neighborhoods like this or the one I live in. In streets with one-family, two-family houses, nobody sits on the porch.

"Television keeps people inside. They don't sit around on the stoops and porches anymore, passing the time of day. Like when I was a boy we still had outhouses where I lived over to the Back of the Yards. If you didn't see your neighbor outside on the porch, you saw him walking back to the outhouse. You said hello. It was friendly."

I could imagine people saying hello on the way to the outhouses. That was Mr. Bikas's memory of better times. Mine was people sitting out on stoops and porches on summer nights. I couldn't imagine what my kids would be looking back on someday saying them was the good old days.

"So you don't need a porch," he goes on. "Maybe you don't need the bays in front. Nobody walks that much anymore. Who wants to sit in a bay and watch the cars go by? Only old people who got nothing else to do. You got plenty to do. Besides, houses nowadays are built facing the back yards. So maybe we put the living room in the back with a nice bay, you could look out on a garden."

I can tell that Mary can see the garden.

Bikas takes out a stub of pencil and turns to a blank page at the back of the album. He starts sketching out a house, keeping up a steady stream of chatter and explanation.

"Here we got the entrance. A little hall big enough for a guest closet and a staircase going upstairs. We make it two steps down into the living room. That makes it feel a little grand, you understand what I'm saying? Over here the kitchen. Big. Like this one. You should have room for a table and chairs. Who needs with these lousy little breakfast nooks? Make the kitchen big and the hell with the dining room. Are you going to want to waste all that space on a room you use twice, maybe three times a year? On holidays and when the in-laws come to visit? You know what I mean? Unless you're very social. Unless you entertain people for dinner a lot."

"The people we have over for dinner would just as soon eat in the kitchen," I says.

"There you go. Dining rooms are foolish. So I give you a nice pantry in the kitchen. You could walk into it."

Bikas is a talker. He's making the sketch he's drawing with this stubby little pencil clutched in his stubby little hand come right up off the page. I can practically see it.

"Over here the living room, in the back. Down this hall the guest room. You don't want guests, you use it to store junk. Everybody's got ten tons of junk nowadays. They ain't using it, but maybe they'll want it someday. It's too good to throw away. So they got no place to put it. Take my advice. Never mind the guests, keep this room for junk. Unless you have so many kids you need the extra room. Then you toss the junk in the garage, leave your car on the street. Who puts their car in the garage anymore?"

By the time he finishes drawing the second floor, any ideas Mike might've put in my head about actually doing some of the building myself goes out the window.

"So," Bikas says, like he's just pushed a truck uphill, "that's that. You want me to handle permits, you want to handle permits? You want me to pick the subcontractors, you want to pick the subcontractors?"

"What are we looking at here, Stavros?" Mike asks.

"You do the permits and subs, this and that, you're looking at a saving of maybe twenty percent. House costs a hundred thousand if I do it all, costs you eighty, maybe eighty-five you do that donkey work yourself."

"Well, that's okay, then," Mike says, "Jim's walking around all day anyway. He could do it on the way here and there."

"Sure," Bikas says, and he grins like he knows something even Mike don't know.

"How long before we can have some drawings so James can start getting the permit?" Mary asks.

"Two, three days."

"How can you do it so fast?" I asks.

"Easy. I save all the drawings of every house I ever worked on. I copy this part of one, that part of another. Put it all together, run it through the blueprint machine. All the specs are boilerplate. Every house is special when it's finished, but in the beginning they're pretty much all alike."

# 11

The next day is more of the same. There's still trouble in the sewer and reclamation system, though I don't have to go down and walk it again.

The next day we find the problem.

It's been four days since I last visited Delvin, so I go over to Larkspur on my lunch hour. I don't wait until two o'clock because I'm feeling guilty about letting it go so long.

I can see how somebody with a sick relative could find excuses not to go visit. It's such a sad thing to have to do.

It looks like it could rain. The sky's gray and flat, and there's that smell of dust in the air.

This time there's no residents sitting out on the enclosed side porch watching television, but I see the big black man, Robert, sitting behind the desk reading a comic book.

His lips are moving, and I get the idea that he's having a hell of a time following the story. I've got to clear my throat before he knows I'm there.

"You cut yourself shaving?" I says, meaning the scar on his face.

When he grins, he practically blinds me.

"No offense," I add.

"Hey, mon, I like de way you come right out wid it. Mos' people take one look at me and dey so skeered dey try to look ever'where excep' at mah face. I get dis cut from a razor, sure enough, but not whilst I was shavin'."

"I come to visit."

"Visitin' hours not till two o'clock. De old people havin' to eat now."

"So I don't think my friend Delvin'll mind if I sit with him while he has his lunch."

"Maybe he don' min', but de front office min's, you know?"

"Anybody in the front office I could talk to?"

"No, dey's havin' dere lunch, too."

"So you're the man in charge?"

"Dat right. I'm de mon."

"You from Haiti?"

"I from Trinidad."

"Nice and warm in Trinidad. No cold winters like here in Chicago."

"Oh, mon, you bring back sweet memories."

"Ever think about going home for a visit?"

"Ver' expensive, dat."

I take a ten-dollar bill out of my pocket and put it on the desk.

Something happens to his eyes. They ain't very friendly anymore.

"You t'ink you can buy de black mon for a ten-dollar bill?"

"I just want you to let me go back and see my friend without bothering the whole establishment."

"I could lose my job I let you go wanderin' aroun' on your own."

I take out another ten and marry it to the one already on the desk.

"I should be insulted you offer me money, but I got to t'ink you don' know no better. What kind of employ-ee would I be if I tol' you to break de rules? What kind of employ-ee would dat make me?"

He drops his comic book on the floor and bends hisself in half reaching for it. "Now, where in de hell dat funny book go?" he says.

I hurry on down the corridor and make the left. I go past some French doors to a dining room. I stop and sneak a look around the door frame. I see there's only a few patients eating in there. All the rest of the people having lunch look like staff. Miss Evergreen is sitting with a man with gray hair who's got his back to me. She glances up, and I duck back.

I go on down the hall and find Delvin's room. I knock on the door to warn him somebody's coming, and I go right in. He ain't in his bed. He's sitting in one of these high chairs with wheels, which Mary tells me is a geriatric chair, staring out the closed window at the garden. But from the look on his face I don't think he even sees the garden.

The smell of neglect and unwashed feet and pee fills my nose. There's a lunch tray sitting on the table next to him. The food on the plate is drying around the edges, and it don't smell too good, either.

I say hello and should I open the window. He don't even let on that I'm in the room while I try to open the window and let in a little air. The window's stuck and won't even budge.

"Ought to tell them to get the maintenance man up here, unstick this window," I says.

Delvin's eyelids flicker a little bit, but that's all I get.

I pull his chair around so he's facing me when I sit on the bed.

"We had a spill down around Eckersall Stadium," I says. "Some kind of waste, salty as hell. Thought for a while there it could be toxic. Guess what we find out it is?"

Delvin just stares past my shoulder at the wall. I pat him on the cheek like he's a baby, I'm trying to get its attention, and he finally focuses his eyes on me.

"So, anyway, we go down around the reclamation plant. Have a little look around. Trace it back. What do you think? There's this old factory used to make pickles. Been closed—I don't know—ten years. Nobody in the building for ten years. There's these gigantic vats where they cure the pickles. Hooked up one after the other. So, what do you think? Ten years ago they forget or don't bother to empty them when they close the doors. Brine eats through the outlet valves one after the other. Whammo! They all let go and spill a couple thousand gallons of the saltiest water in Chicago right into the sewers. Ain't that something?"

He opens his mouth and moves his jaw up and down. For a

minute I think he's going to say something. But all he wants is some water.

When I fill up a plastic cup from a plastic pitcher on the bedside table and hold it for him while he drinks, I can see he ain't wearing his dentures. Just one tooth in his bottom jaw sticks up like a broken tusk. I wonder why a person would leave just one tooth in his mouth that way, but I suppose it's like a sign of youth and strength and he don't want to let it go.

"Hey, Chips, what's going on here?" I says. "What've they done to you?"

The door opens up, and Evergreen walks in with a tall guy, around fifty, right behind her. It's the gray-haired character she was having lunch with.

"Mr. Flannery," she says, almost managing to cluck her tongue. "What do you think you're doing in here?"

"I'm here to see how my friend is doing, and it don't look to me like he's doing too good."

"He's been sedated. He had a restless night, and at his age, especially in his weakened condition, sleep is essential. I don't suppose a doctor's ever told you that people—especially older people—are particularly vulnerable to all sorts of illness after suffering a tragedy?"

"I don't know if keeping him zonked out is the way to build up his health," I says, getting off the bed and going around Delvin's chair to face her.

"Don't you think that should be left up to the medical experts?" the man says.

"Are you a medical expert?"

He smiles like he's amused at the notion and shakes his head as though I've said something very witty. "I trust them, though," he says, in this superior way.

"Well, see, I don't necessarily do. I don't trust the kind of care they provide around here, either. So I'm not talking about medical theories. I'm talking about a hot room with a window what won't open and an old man what stares out the window without seeing anything and smells like he ain't been washed in three days."

Evergreen pulls herself up like she's ready to call me outside to fight it out. "Mr. Flannery," she says, biting my name off like the name was my head, "how would you like it if I came down to your office and asked you why the floor wasn't swept or the walls painted or a broken valve was lying on your desk in the middle of your paperwork? How'd you like it if you were working one place and I came along and asked you why you weren't taking care of something someplace else? How'd you like it if I give you a hard time when you was in the middle of your goddam work, trying to make what you had stretch to do three times the work?"

While she's giving me hell her language changes. She starts off lecturing me like an educated person and ends up telling me off like somebody from the Back of the Yards.

"Come in and volunteer your time, Flannery. Get the state to cough up a little more money for the welfare patients and tell them to stop dumping mentals on us claiming they're just old. Get me a budget so I can pay my staff a decent wage."

"Hey," I says, trying to stop the flood. "We're not talking about a sanitation office here, we're talking about a nursing home. We're not talking about a valve sitting on my desk but an old man sitting in his own mess."

"I know what we're talking about. I'm dealing with it every day. I'm telling you that we're doing the best we can. Your friend's being evaluated, his condition stabilized, his apprehensions put to rest." She's talking fancy again. "When he's fit, he'll be moved into a room with another patient. He'll be brought into the regular schedule of things."

"No, he won't, because I'm taking him out of here with me as soon as I can find his clothes."

"Look, Flannery," the tall man says, moving between Evergreen and me, crowding my face, "I suppose you're used to making trouble—"

"How's that?"

"I've heard a lot about you. You seem to run around sticking your nose into matters that don't concern you. Making mountains out of molehills."

"Get out of my way before I step on your foot and spoil your shoeshine."

Delvin groans and starts to whine.

"I ain't got time to discuss my reputation," I says. "I'm taking Mr. Delvin out of here."

"I doubt that," the tall jaboney says, and he looks me up and down like he's ready to step on me and squash me like a bug.

"You're not saying you're ready to fight me on that, are you?" I asks.

He shakes his head and grins like I'm really cracking his funny bone.

"I can have a court order inside of thirty minutes," I says, threatening him with political clout, which is something I don't like to do but which I will do if it'll save me time and trouble on the front end.

"I'm sure you could spend a favor and get it done, but it won't do you a bit of good. I'm in the process of having myself declared Cousin Frank's legal guardian even as we speak."

"Cousin Frank?"

"My name's Francis Carmody. I was named after Cousin Frank."

"How's that?"

"My mother and father named me for Cousin Frank."

"If they knew him very good they'd know nobody calls him Frank and he hates the name Francis. Everybody who knows him even a little calls him Chips or Mr. Delvin."

"Except family, Flannery. Except family," Carmody says, like he's handing me the fatal zinger.

"So, what's the relation?" I says, having nothing better to say at the moment and needing to say something even though it makes me feel like a kid playing double dare in the playground.

"Frank's grandmother on her mother's side, Roseann, had five children by her fourth husband, Aloysius Flynn. The eldest, Clara, married Frank's father, Martin Delvin. The youngest, Belle, married Michael Carmody. They were my grandparents. Their son, William Carmody, is my father. Deceased, as is my mother."

"God rest their souls."

"Thank you for the blessing," Carmody says. "So, have I convinced you of my right as Cousin Frank's nearest relative to take the responsibility for his welfare?"

"If it all checks out, I'd say you got the legal right. Then I'd tell you to start taking better care."

"And I'd tell you thanks for the advice but it's no concern of yours. Take care of your business, Mr. Flannery, and I'll take care of mine."

While they're seeing me to the door I catch a glimpse of Agnes Spencer. She's peering out at me from behind a sick-looking potted palm, clutching her chenille robe to her skinny neck.

Evergreen sees her and peels off to shoo her back into her room while Carmody walks me the rest of the way to the front door, where he shakes my hand and sticks a pen in my pocket.

"Brand new item," he says.

It ain't quite the bum's rush, but it's the next thing to it.

Out on the sidewalk I take a look at the pen. It's one of them novelty pens with a little woman in a bathing suit. When you turn it upside down she goes through a barrel and the bathing suit comes off.

# 12

I go home early because Mary's changed shifts and Bikas's delivered the house plans, and this way we'll have the late afternoon to talk over any changes we could want before she has to go to work.

There's eight sheets of drawings what show the floor plan, the elevations, the roofing scheme, the electrical layout, and this and that.

Years ago, when I was only a kid, I went over with my father to help a pal of his, Joe Harrigan, build a house at Sansone Slough, which is west of Chicago, almost at the border of Cook and Will counties, and which is surrounded by forest.

I remember it was a nice sunny day when they stood around on this empty piece of land and talked about what they was going to do.

"Well, Dotty's first up in the morning, and she's going to want the kitchen facing the east so she can get the sun," Joe says.

"And you're going to want to sit on the porch and watch the sun go down when you get home from work," Mike says, "so here's the steps and the railing along here." He scrapes a line on the dirt with the heel of his shoe. "You going to have a dining room?"

"I couldn't care one way or the other," Joe says, "but Dotty says we got to have one because her sister's got one, and she don't want her sister looking down her nose at her because we eat in the kitchen."

"You're probably going to eat in the kitchen anyway."

"So, that's all right, we can use the dining room for an extra bedroom if we got to down the line."

"So it better be out of the way across a hall instead of right next to the kitchen," my father says.

"That's a good idea. With a toilet and a sink in a room next to it."

"Don't need a lot of space for that. How about right next to the back door?"

"Off the mud porch. Okay."

"Two bedrooms upstairs to start?"

"That's all we'll need by the time the house's built unless Dotty's not telling me something," Joe says, and they both laugh, though I don't see anything funny about it.

"Stairs here," Mike says, "right in line with the front entrance, so the kids' bedroom better be back here so they can't go roaming around at night without they got to pass your bedroom and you'll hear them."

"Living room," Joe says, standing still on a mound of grass.

"Got your nicest view out this way," Mike says, spreading his arms and standing with his back to the stand of trees about a quarter of a mile away.

Why he picks out them particular trees with trees all around the place is beyond me, but I'm so interested in the way they're doing what they're doing that I don't even bother to ask.

"So that's it, ain't it?" Mike says, going over to a spot and kicking a hole in the ground with his heel. "Here's the corner of your living room."

Joe goes over with a wooden stake and a six-pound hammer and knocks the stake into the ground, and that's how they started building a house.

Looking over the plans of the house Mary and me is going to build, I got a feeling it's going to be a lot harder than that for us.

After I make some eggs for supper and Mary goes off to work, I go over to the office Janet Canarias keeps open two nights a week so she can do pro bono work for the people in the neighborhood what can't afford a lawyer.

It's the same storefront she used when she ran for alderman and won. It's still being donated by the citizen's committee what urged her to go for the job, otherwise she probably couldn't make the rent. She's been waiting for the landlord to ask for his quid pro quo.

You get to learn a lot of Latin hanging around politics, but, in plain English, it always comes down to favor for favor.

"Well, Fidel asked for his payoff," she says as I sit down in the client's chair alongside her desk.

"A little favor down at the building department? A little something about condemning a building he wants to buy?"

"A little piece of me."

"What're you telling me? He knows your persuasion. It was practically what won you the election."

"I don't know about that, but anyway he tells me he can change my mind."

"He's fat, bald, and sixty."

"He thinks I probably have a thing for my father, my grandfather, that's never been resolved." She grins.

"What'd you tell him?"

"I told him he could be right, but that I'd have to give it a lot of thought. I figure I can stall a final answer for at least a year. That way I won't have to say no to condemning any buildings or tell him I can't close my eyes to any irregularities he might have planned by way of doing business. And by that time my private practice might be doing well enough for me to afford to pay the rent on an office."

"Or you'll have enough legitimate favors in your bank you can get it on a deal."

Her grin turns a little wry. "It looks like you and me are about the only ones around willing to do something for nothing," she says.

"I don't know about that," I says. "We all got to get something out of what we do even if it's mostly a good feeling. I remember one day when I was a baby. I crawl out of my playpen and bite the cat. When my mother—God rest her soul—puts me back behind the bars she says, 'Now, be a good boy and it's mashed peaches for supper.' So already there's a deal. Favor for favor. I don't bite the cat and I get peaches."

"Jimmy," she says, making a face like she knows I'm putting her on.

"Well, I didn't bite the cat no more. What my mother don't know is that after one taste of that cat I ain't planning on biting it again anyways."

"I don't know if you're a cynic or a saint," Janet says.

"The point is, there's nothing wrong with making contracts— as long as you keep them—or trading favor for favor—as long as everybody keeps the accounts straight. It's what makes the world go 'round."

She grins again, showing these perfect white teeth in this beautiful brown face.

"How's your old friend Delvin?" she asks.

"He don't look good to me, and I don't like that place he's in."

"What's it called?"

"The Larkspur. Over in the Fourteenth. You hear about it?"

She shakes her head. "No, but then why would I if it's over in the Fourteenth?"

"No complaints about it on the grapevine?"

"You're closer to the vine than I am."

"So, nothing?"

"I can call Hilda Moscowitz. Being alderman in the Fourteenth, she'd know about any irregularities or illegalities if anybody'd know."

"I don't know if what I got to complain about is strong enough."

"What's bothering you?"

"I think they dress the front of the house like it was a restaurant, you know what I mean? They put clean, shiny old folks out there on the closed-in porch watching color television. Trot out a few into the dining room for lunch and dinner if any strangers are around. Put the newcomers and the paying customers in nice rooms because they figure the friends and relatives'll come around pretty often at first and then stop coming around so much. Then they move them to rooms in the back and upstairs which they don't keep so clean and tidy, you know what I mean?"

"What kind of evidence can you provide?"

"All anybody's got to do is go take a look."

"Like somebody from Human Services?"

"If that's the office to do the job."

"I don't know what good it'll do. They can't respond to every complaint from a disgruntled son or daughter, husband or wife. They haven't got the manpower to cover every unsubstantiated complaint. I mean they'd get around to it when they could get around to it, but by that time the word would've gone out that they were going to have a look, and the facility would have plenty of time to clean up its act."

"So that'd be something, at least."

"But not nearly enough. Besides . . ."

"Besides what?"

"I've heard about complaints like that being made, and when the social services go into the suspected facility they can't find anything to get them for. Later on they've found out that the helpless relative of the complaining party suffers for it."

"Catch twenty-two. Let things go like they're going and somebody suffers. Complain to see if you can make things better and somebody suffers more."

"We can start an investigation, Jimmy. I could get Hilda Moscowitz and some other aldermen behind me on it. But we'd have to have something more than your bad feelings about the place."

"What kind of evidence would you want?"

"If any of the employees were willing to testify, that might be enough to start. The trouble with that, though, is probably most of them are either illegals or unemployable nearly anywhere else. So who's going to blow the whistle and lose a job?"

"Ain't there anybody watching what goes on?"

"Sure. That's part of the reason for dressing the set. In case there's a snap inspection. How many snap inspections you think they get in a year? People make deals. People send warnings. That's the downside of favor for favor."

I sit there for a minute trying to work it out in my head. How to get through and around the corruption and the deals that collect around money-making schemes like barnacles on a sewer outlet into the lake. No light bulbs pop on, so I figure I better ask what I came to ask and think about what I'm going to do about getting Delvin out of Larkspur later on.

"You could do me a small favor?" I says.

"Tell me."

"Could you make a phone call and find out if one Francis Carmody has been appointed Delvin's conservator? Could you ask around first thing in the morning?"

"I can do better than that," she says, reaching for the phone and punching in a number. "I've got a friend who's the chief clerk in Chancery Court. He works late, and he's got a memory like an elephant."

She smiles and nods at me when somebody picks up on the other end.

"Hector? Janet Canarias. I need a favor. Sure, I know the drill. Favor for favor. But this is a very small favor, Hector. It doesn't rate a night out. No. I tell you what. If you have a pretty sister, maybe she and I can have dinner. That way you'll at least keep it in the family. No, no, Hector, you must believe me when I tell you I'm not good for men. Maybe someday. You know what the politicians say, 'Never say never.'"

She listens for a little bit, smiling and nodding and shaking her head while I sit there thinking what a beautiful woman and nice person she is and how, if I wasn't married and I met somebody like her, I'd be frustrated as hell because she liked women more than men.

"I'd like to know if one Francis Carmody has been named conservator and guardian for one—" She raises her eyebrows at me.

"Francis," I says.

"—Francis Delvin, aged male."

She grins and snaps her fingers, telling me that this Hector don't even have to look it up. He's got it all in his head.

"Thank you, Hector. If I ever decide to change my style, you'll be one of the first to know."

"Carmody has been so named," she says, holding her hand over the mouthpiece.

"Ask him who signed the affidavit swearing to Carmody's identity and relationship to Delvin."

She asks Hector the question.

"Wallace Dunleavy," she tells me.

# 13

The next thing I figure I got to do about the house is go over to get a water meter at the Water Service Bureau, which I don't think is going to be too difficult. So I put Alfie in the car and go over to South Sacramento. I park the car and let Alfie out so he can lie under it and get plenty of fresh air and shade while I'm gone.

Water Service's a big office with lots of people waiting to do business. I get in the information line.

It takes maybe twenty minutes, half an hour, for me to step up to the counter and to this lady with blue hair who's sitting on a stool the other side of it. Just as I open my mouth she pulls a sign what says "Closed" from underneath the counter and slaps it in front of me. Keeping her eyes on me—she shouldn't miss an ounce of my frustration—she slides off the stool and walks away.

Ten minutes later she's back and climbs up on the stool, still giving me the look. It ain't enough I don't complain, she's got to rub it in.

"When you got to go, you got to go," I says, giving her a smile.

"What?" she says.

"I understand all about that, being I'm a sanitary engineer," I says, figuring I'll show the flag so she'll know we're in the same civil service army.

"A plumber?" she asks, not getting it.

"A sewer inspector," I says.

"Whattaya know," she says. "What can I do for you?"

"I'm going to build a house, and I'll need a water meter."

"Sure you will. Here's the form you got to fill out. When you finish you can get in that line over there or you can send it in by mail."

"If I fill it out now, will it speed things up?"

"It could, but there's no promises. Processing takes two, three weeks, no matter how your application gets into the office. So you mail it, maybe it takes a day, maybe two days. So, let's say two days. This is Wednesday. Maybe it gets here Friday. Before noon, that's good. After one, that's not so good. Nobody starts the process— you understand what I'm telling you?—if it comes in after lunch on Friday. It waits till Monday. Say you already lost a week."

"So maybe I better fill it out right now," I says.

"You got the time, that'd be good."

I go over and start filling out the application when Carmody's pen runs out of ink before I even finish my name.

I go back to the information desk and sort of lean in a little so the guy who's up there asking questions'll know I'm not getting pushy but that what I got to ask won't take but a second.

"Take your place in line," the lady with the blue hair snaps.

"I just wanted to ask if I could borrow a pen."

"We don't supply pens."

"My pen ran out of ink. All I want to do is borrow a pen for a minute."

"Get back in line and make your request when your turn comes."

"But I was just in line and—"

The next guy in line hands me one of seven or eight pens he's got clipped to this plastic card what protects his pocket. You can see he's a professional at this game.

"Here's a pen," he says.

"Thanks. I'll get it right back to you."

"Keep it. You're building a house, maybe you'll need a plumber. I'd be glad to trade you numbers."

"Trade me numbers?"

"Bid the job. I'll take a set of plans and tell you what it'll cost you if I put in the pipes, sinks, toilets, and whatever."

"I know what is 'bid the job.' It was 'trade the numbers' that threw me."

"You're new at this, right?"

"First time."

"I'll bet it's your only time."

"How's that?"

"You got a job with the city, ain't that what I heard you tell Mabel here?"

"Hello, Mabel," I says.

"You're holding up the line," Mabel says.

I look at the pen the man gives me. It's got his name and business printed on the barrel. "Duke the Plumber."

"That's right, Duke, I work for the city."

"It's better than being a contractor. Take it from me. So go ahead, keep the pen."

I go back to the application and finish filling it out. There's some blanks I don't know what to do with, but I figure the clerk sitting next to Mabel, who'll be looking over the application, should know the answers.

So it's maybe half an hour, forty minutes before I step up in front of him just as he takes the same "Closed" sign and puts it on the counter in front of me.

"Hey, you going to do what you got to do, too?" I asks.

"Ten-thirty," he says. "It's my coffee break."

Before I can say anything to that, he's gone over to a desk in the corner where he's got a thermos and a brown bag waiting. I watch him while he drinks his coffee and eats his bun. I got the feeling I'm in a post office, if you know what I mean.

In fifteen minutes he's back, wiping the crumbs out of his mustache.

"So," he says as he starts looking over my application, "Mr. Flannery, is it?"

"You heard of me?" I says hopefully, figuring if this fellow city worker's ever heard of me he might remember I'm the guy what did a good deed for Baby, the gorilla over to the zoo, what is the sweetheart of the entire city.

He jerks back like I just accused him of something.

"Who said I ever heard of you?" he practically yells.

"Mr. Kepski never heard of you," Mabel says.

"How do you know that?" I asks. "Do you sit around all day asking each other who you know, who you don't know? How could you know who he knows?"

"I'm Mrs. Kepski," she says.

"Oh."

"And I don't know you. If I don't know you, he don't know you. And if he don't know you, we don't know you."

What am I supposed to say? Here I am, practically in a fight, because I ask a clerk does he happen to know me. So I shut my mouth.

"You got a business license?" Kepski asks me.

"What do I need with a business license?"

"Because you're going into business."

"No, I'm not. I'm just going to build a house."

"That's a business enterprise."

"No, it's not. I'm building a house for myself and my wife."

"Not for resale?"

"No. To live in."

"So you don't need a contractor's license, but you still need a business license."

"This is the only time I'm ever going to build a house."

"You never know."

"I know."

"I mean we don't know that for sure. You could build a house and then another house and then another house and always say you're just building one house. Not for resale."

"All right. I need a license. You mind telling me why I need the license?"

"Because the city wants your hundred and fifty bucks," Duke the Plumber says.

"I just paid two hundred and fifty down at Building Permits."

"We got nothing to do with Building," Kepski says. "This is a business license you need because you got to hire people to build your house."

"Okay. So give me a business license."

He looks at me like he doubts my sanity. "You can't get a business license here."

"So where do I get a business license?"

"Department of Revenue. One twenty-one north LaSalle. When you got your business license, come back here."

I swear the two people sitting side by side, perched on stools behind the counter at New Business Licenses, could be the brother and sister of Mr. and Mrs. Kepski.

She's got blue hair and a wicked smile. He's got rimless glasses and a mustache.

They're a little more organized at Revenue. They've got the applications waiting in a wooden box, and you can take one for yourself without standing in line. Also I still got Duke the Plumber's pen, which ain't run out of ink. So I'm on top of it.

When I get up to the counter and hand over the application I can't help asking, "You happen to know a husband and wife, works over to where you get the water meters, by the name of Kepski?"

He gives me the old one-eye and says, "Why would I know anybody named Kepski?"

"You and the lady sitting next to you look enough like Mr. and Mrs. Kepski to be brothers and sisters."

"What's going on here, Harold?" this second lady with blue hair says.

"This guy wants to know do we know any Kepskis."

"I know a Lipshitz over to a hundred and fifth."

"This guy's name is Flannery," he says, shoving his thumb at me.

She frowns and nods like that tells it all.

"Look, Mr. Flannery, you want a business license, is that it?"

"That's it."

"You know you got to go to the office of Personal Income Tax Withholding if you expect to pay any one worker more than a hundred dollars a week?"

"I didn't know that. Is it going to cost me?"

"Well, you got to deduct the personal income tax. Also you got to pay disability insurance, unemployment insurance tax, and employment training tax."

"I'm just building this one house for myself and my wife, and I'm never going to build another," I says.

"So why don't you get a contractor to do the whole thing for you?"

"Because then I probably couldn't afford the house. I'm trying to save a little money here by doing the running around for permits, licenses, and subcontractors myself."

I'd say the man has the decency to smile, except I don't like the way the smile looks.

"By the way, has anybody told you that you've got to get a workman's compensation insurance policy?"

"Where would I get one of those?"

"Well, not here."

I wander out with nothing accomplished and half the day shot wondering how houses ever get built by anybody except professionals and why even professionals would want to go through it.

"You wouldn't believe it, Alfie," I says.

He looks at me like he's ready to believe anything I got to tell him.

"The red tape you got to go through makes a dish of spaghetti look like a dish of rulers."

He licks his nose with his tongue.

"Unless," I says, the dawn sneaking up over the swamp I call a brain.

Alfie cocks his head like he's saying, unless what?

"Things is bad but not impossible until they catch a gander at my name. Then all of a sudden mud turns to granite, you know what I mean? You don't suppose Dunleavy is giving me a little reminder that he told me to lay off nosing around the Larkspur?"

Alfie gives a little yelp. He knows Dunleavy's reputation for having things his way as good as I do.

# 14

I'm lying in bed and I can't sleep.

I'm worrying about Delvin in the nursing home.

I'm worrying about maybe I'll have to bite the bullet and either let them shove me up the ladder in the party or get out. You can't keep on turning down promotions before people get sick and tired of offering.

I'm worrying about leaving the flat and the neighborhood.

I can't say that where we live on Polk ain't starting to get a little frayed around the edges. There's no young lawyers or stockbrokers coming in buying the old three-flats and six-flats and turning them into magazine covers like they're doing in other parts of the city. But it's my neighborhood, and I don't want to give it up.

But we already talked with Mr. Bikas, and we got the set of plans he made on his blueprint machine, and I'm already learning a little bit how to handle myself walking through the ocean of red tape.

If we had a house, Mary would maybe have a kid. Maybe she'd stop working for a while.

But if we go ahead, I'm going to have to take out a loan to build the place. Mike says he'll help me. He's got a little money put away I can have for start-up money, and he'll cosign the loan, and I can get plenty of references. Maybe.

Also Mike's been going on about how he helped Joe Harrigan

build his house. He says if I want, he'll actually swing a hammer alongside me, and we'll put most of the structure up by ourselves. On weekends and holidays, he says.

He's got the wrong man. I can change a light bulb, but I wouldn't trust myself for much more than that.

Also I can already tell I'm going to be so busy filling out papers I couldn't find time to swing a hammer if I wanted to.

I'm lying there staring at the ceiling. It's three o'clock in the morning, and I'm worrying about making changes in my life. I'm not a great one for change. Mike says that's a sign that I'm getting old. Older than him even.

Mary stirs alongside me. The next thing I know she's half-awake, putting her head on my shoulder and her arm across my chest.

"James, love," she says, "you don't have to be a committeeman if you don't want to."

"I didn't mean to wake you up."

"You don't have to run for alderman. You don't have to try for Mr. Delvin's job now that the poor old soul's over the hill. And we don't have to build a house on that lot Mrs. Banjo left you. We can live right here forever and ever, and I promise you I won't complain about the paint or stairs or plumbing more than once a week until we're ninety."

I give her a kiss alongside her eye and ask her did I shuffle around and wake her up.

"It's when you're as still as an old bone that I wake up," she says, drowsy as a kitten. "Don't lie so quiet."

The phone rings out in the kitchen right then.

We ain't got a phone in the bedroom because if it's for me I got ears like a bat and I don't want it waking Mary up at odd hours when she works all these different shifts over to Passavant and needs her sleep.

I slip out from under the covers and put on my robe, thinking that if I'm worried about her sleep I got to learn to move around a little when I'm wide awake in bed. I go out into the kitchen. Alfie gives me the old one-eye from the place where he sleeps by the stove.

When I pick up the receiver and say hello, nobody answers.

"It's three o'clock in the morning," I says. "If this is a heavy breather, I got to tell you you didn't get lucky playing dial roulette. I ain't some woman you can scare to death."

There's some mumbling and lisping I can't understand. The connection ain't the best, and whoever's on the line is having some kind of trouble speaking up.

"I can't hear you. You better—"

I hear somebody say what sounds like, "Flannery?"

"Who's this?"

Then I hear somebody yelling in the distance on the other end. "Mama, mama, mama, they got me tied down. They won't let me scratch my nose. Mama, mama, get me loose. I'll be a good girl forever."

The person on the other end hangs up.

I didn't hear enough of the person whispering on the bad line to make book on it, but with that lady yelling to be let loose in the background, I'd be willing to bet the house I ain't even built yet that it was Delvin calling me.

When I go back into the bedroom and start getting dressed Mary asks me what the call was all about.

I tell her I can't be sure, but I think it was Delvin, and he sounded like he was in some distress.

"Are you going over there at this hour?" she asks, sitting up with her eyes still only half open.

"I don't know what else I can do."

"You might call the Larkspur and ask them if anything's wrong."

"At this hour of the morning? It could be I'm mistaken. It could be the old man woke up and didn't know where he was or what time it was and thought he'd just give me a call."

"Then call the police and have them drive by and see if there's any unusual activity at the nursing home."

"I bother them and they'll say, 'There goes that Jimmy Flannery sticking his nose in again.'"

"Make an anonymous complaint."

By this time I'm dressed. All I got left to put on is my shoes.

"You're going over there no matter what I say, aren't you?" she says.

"I'm not being stubborn," I says. "It's just that I got to have a look or I'll never get to sleep."

She don't argue anymore.

"Go ahead, run around in the middle of the night if it suits you. But take care of yourself. As long as you're going out, you might as well take Alfie for a walk."

I give her a kiss and tuck the covers in around her chin.

Out in the hall, Alfie's standing by the door wagging his tail, having heard his name and the word "walk."

We trot downstairs, keeping it quiet, and I unlock my car, which is standing at the curb. Alfie jumps in.

There's very little traffic on the streets. The city's asleep except for a couple of street people shuffling along the gutters, a prowl car, and a garbage truck going somewhere.

When I pull up in front of the Larkspur and look it over, it looks pretty peaceful. There's a light on in the vestibule, which I suppose is for ordinary security reasons, according to city ordinance. I get out of the car, figuring I'll just walk around once.

"Come on out here, Alfie," I says. "I'm going to be a man walking his dog. You see a squirrel or something, keep it down. Okay?"

We walk up the path toward the porch and around the side so I can look in through the windows of the glassed-in porch and see if there's anybody at the desk. Somebody's sitting there, but their back's to me, and I can't even tell if the night attendant is a man or a woman.

I keep on going around toward the back with Alfie at my heels. The ducks is murmuring to themselves back at the pond. I look over there and see something white lying on the ground, like a newspaper or a white coat.

"Keep it quiet," I says again.

He gives me a look like he's telling me he ain't that dumb.

I walk closer and closer to whatever the bundle is. The closer I get the worse I start to feel. Twenty steps away I can see it ain't newspaper. Fifteen feet away I can see it ain't an empty coat. Ten feet away I can see it's somebody lying facedown on the grass and the ornamental stones with their face in the pond.

Whoever it is has got on an old worn chenille robe. I'm afraid it's that lady I met in the hall who talked about mice. Mrs. Spencer.

I squat down and bend my head sideways to look at her face. I see it ain't a her. It's a him. Mr. Custer's the person lying there with his face turned to the side and his nose in the water.

The ducks have already started nibbling at his hair.

They try to come back and squawk like devils when I shoo them away.

# 15

After I make double sure Mr. Custer's dead, I go up to the door of the Larkspur Nursing Home and ring the bell. I got to push the button three or four times before the night attendant gets up from the desk, comes to the door, turns on another security light on the porch, and peers through the clear spots in the pattern on the frosted glass.

I have to tell her three times that one of their patients is dead, lying facedown in the pond, before she goes to wake up Evergreen.

When Evergreen comes striding across the entry hall in her bathrobe she's got Robert, the Trinidadian, behind her. He's not wearing his white jacket, just sweat pants and a short-sleeved undershirt torn off so his belly's exposed. He's also wearing unlaced running shoes. He looks twice as big and three times as mean as he did sitting behind the desk.

After I glance at his feet I look at Evergreen's, and I notice she's wearing stockings under her slippers.

Evergreen opens the door and says, "What's this about somebody dead, Mr. Flannery?" like she's a sergeant and I'm one of her soldiers. She's got a flashlight in her hand and flicks it on, shining it in my face, acting like she'd like to shoot the messenger for bringing bad news or like she thinks I could be drunk and playing a joke on her. Then she spots Alfie and says, "What's that?"

"That's my dog, Alfie," I says.

"Your dog?" she says, like she's saying, "Your accomplice."

"I figured I was going out anyway, I might as well give Alfie a little walk."

"Why were you out in the first place, Mr. Flannery?"

"Ms. Evergreen," I says, "it's the middle of the night when I get this call from somebody. I can't make out what he's trying to tell me, but I think it's my friend, Delvin."

She walks past me and down the steps, lighting her way with the flash. I trot after her.

"So you got out of bed in the small hours of the morning and came all the way across the city to check us out?"

"Don't make it sound like I'm just some fool with a long nose and nothing better to do than prowl around in the dark," I says, all the time walking around the house and across the back yard toward the pond—me scooting alongside Evergreen, who's practically running, with the Trinidadian and the woman attendant right behind us. "I've got a natural concern for a friend and a natural curiosity about telephone calls in the middle of the night."

"Oh," she yelps, and she pulls up short, having got a gander at the old man with his face in the water, the ducks all over him again, pecking away. She sort of staggers, and I put an arm around her so she shouldn't fall.

"I was trying to warn you, Ms. Evergreen," I says.

She looks at me and says, "Lenore. My name's Lenore, Mr. Flannery." It's like she thinks if she can turn the situation into a social event, the dead body and the ducks'll go away.

"My name's Jimmy, Lenore, but that's neither here or there."

"Robert," she snaps.

He starts moving to pull the body out of the water like she'd give him an order. The movement scares the ducks, and they go flapping and squawking out of the way, angry at being interrupted at their picnic again.

"I wouldn't touch it," I says, and Robert stops where he is, half bending over, his head turned over his shoulder, looking first at me and then at his boss.

"We can't leave her lying there with her face in the water like that," Lenore says.

"We can't do anything else until the police come."

"At least let me see who she is."

"It ain't a she, Lenore. It's Mr. Custer."

She starts to bend down to have a look like she can't believe what I just said and has to see for herself.

"If you got to look, I wouldn't get too close," I says. "I already muddled around in there to make sure he was really dead, and the more people slog around the less chance Forensics will have to find any footprints or other evidence."

She squats down, staying well back, and shines the light on the old man's face. She gasps when she sees what the ducks've done and sits down on the wet grass. Her robe falls open, and I can see her stockings are attached to a black lace garter belt.

Robert and me both reach for her at the same time, but Robert wins and gets her on her feet.

"It's Mr. Custer," she says. "Oh, dear."

"Putting it mildly," I says.

"He wanders around in the night sometimes."

I'm about to make some remark about how could he do that when he's locked in most of the time, when I remember she don't know I was prowling around that time on my own. So I keep my mouth shut.

"But somebody always finds him before he gets outside," she goes on.

She looks at the night nurse, who shakes her head vigorously and says, "No, no, no. I looked in on him at two o'clock when I made my rounds, and he was tucked up warm and safe. Sleeping good for a change, as a matter of fact. No way he could've—"

"Got by you?" Evergreen says.

The woman's scared to death. Her hands start to tremble, and her face folds up like a piece of crumpled tissue paper. "He must've found another way out."

"You sure you didn't doze off, Mrs. . . . ?" I says.

"Child," Evergreen says, but she don't really introduce me to the attendant.

"No, no, no," Mrs. Child says again, in the same almost angry way, tossing a look at Robert, who's standing there looking at Evergreen. "I didn't fall asleep."

"I know you didn't nap, Mrs. Child," Evergreen says. "Nobody's going to accuse you of not doing your duty." Then she turns to me and says, "I don't think we know enough about what happened to go pointing the finger at anybody right this minute. We'd better call the police."

"That's a good idea," I says. "The longer we wait to make the call, the longer it'll take for them to get here and the longer Mr. Custer's going to have to lie there with his head in the pond."

I hear a car start up halfway down the block.

"Will you stay here, Mr. Flannery, and keep the ducks away from him?"

"Robert'll have to do it. I'm going to have a look and see is my friend all right."

She hesitates for a minute, but under the circumstances she can't see how she can tell me not to.

"Wait for me, Alfie," I says, and the three of us, Mrs. Child, Evergreen, and me, go trooping back to the house.

"Mrs. Child, will you call the police?" Evergreen says the minute we get inside. "I'm going with Mr. Flannery to check on his friend."

Mrs. Child just stands there, still trembling, her face crumpling up like it did before.

"You better make the call yourself," I says.

Evergreen don't argue with me. She goes into the office to make the call.

I make a beeline for Delvin's room.

He's sleeping okay, his mouth open, the one tooth showing like the fang of a worn-out walrus past the age of fighting.

I stand there for a minute watching him breathe and thinking things over. Thinking about what don't sit right. What nudges and needles the brain.

First of all I wonder what Lenore was thinking of, taking the time to put on stockings when she was roused out of bed at three-thirty in the A.M., unless she never took them off because she wasn't ready for bed. Also the garter belt ain't the kind of underwear I'd expect her to go for.

Second, I wonder how come she's so sturdy and efficient one minute and falling on her ass, when she has a look at Mr. Custer, the next. After all, anybody spends any time around a nursing home gets to see death and sickness in some pretty unpleasant ways. Maybe it was because she didn't expect to see Mr. Custer?

Third, I wonder if Robert always sleeps in his running togs.

Fourth, how come, since I didn't say where I found the body before Lenore went marching off the porch, she turns the corner and knows just where to go?

There could be innocent explanations for every one of them questions. There could be not.

Also there's a couple of questions from the other day. How come Carmody was there when I come back to see Delvin? How come he already knew who I was?

I close the door softly behind me as I leave Delvin's room. I hear a "Pssst!" and when I turn around there's Mrs. Spencer peeking at me from a room down the hall, her nose sticking through the crack and one eye glittering at me.

"Hey you," she whispers. "What's going on?"

I go over to her, and she opens the door a little wider.

"There's been a little trouble," I says.

"What kind of trouble?"

"There's been an accident."

"Talking to you is like pulling teeth," she says. "Get in here."

I go inside, and she shuts the door behind us.

"Keep your voice down," she says. "They don't allow persons of the opposite sex in the rooms with the door closed."

She smiles at the idea that anybody would suspect we were doing things we shouldn't be doing behind closed doors.

"Is something the matter with your friend Delvin?" she asks.

"Why'd you say that?"

"Why'd you be here this time of the morning otherwise?" she says right back, except there's just a little stutter of hesitation, like the reason for my being there just dawned on her that second.

"Mr. Custer . . ." I hesitate.

"What about Charles?" Her face screws up.

"He must've fallen down outside and drowned in the duck pond."

"Jesus, Mary, and Joseph," she says, and she sits down on the edge of her bed. "I should never have lent him my bathrobe."

"How come you did that?"

"Well, Jack Boxer locked him in and took away all his clothes again so Charles wouldn't go wandering. He come knocking at my door tonight."

"If they locked him in, how did he get out of his room?"

"I don't know. The night attendant could've looked in on him and forgot to lock the door when he left."

"Him?"

"Mr. Custer," she says, looking at me as though I'm not too bright.

"No, I mean you called the night attendant a him."

"Sure I did. Robert St. John, the big black fella is on nights this week."

"That his name?"

"Yes, St. John. But he don't pronounce it that way."

"Mrs. Child was at the desk when I rang the bell."

Mrs. Spencer's eyebrows go up. "Oh?"

"What does that mean?" I asks.

"Evergreen looks like she's laced in pretty tight, but there's been whispers that she likes a bit of a wrestle now and then."

"With St. John?"

"Well, you know how whispers don't always get the details right. But why not?"

She smiles like the idea pleases her.

I wonder if this ain't just the kind of mean gossip spread around by people who feel they got no power about people who got the power over them. Still and all, it could fit in with the stockings and garter belt. It could be something to remember.

"So what did Mr. Custer want when he came knocking on your door?" I asks.

"Something to put on, for God's sake. I give him my chenille dressing gown. It's the nicest one I got." Her eyes flick on and off my face like a fly buzzing back and forth. She's scared to death but trying not to show it.

"What'd he need a dressing gown for?" I asks.

"Because he didn't want to go around bare-assed is why," she says, like now she knows I really am brain-stunned.

"Is that all he told you?"

Her eyes get a little wary.

"He just said he wanted something to wear," she says.

I already noticed she ain't got a telephone in her room, so I says, "I see you ain't got a telephone. Did Mr. Custer have a telephone in his room?"

"Only the ones paying plenty to stay here got the luxury of a telephone in the room," she says. "Everybody else's got to use the pay phone in the lobby, and then they'll ask you what the hell you're doing out of bed."

"Is that the only pay phone around?"

"There's one in the day room down the hall, but the door's locked after ten."

"I better be getting back," I says. "The police're on the way. So don't be scared if there's a lot of commotion out in the back yard."

I go to the door and open it. She goes with me and touches my sleeve.

"Do you think it hurt Charles? Dying, I mean," she asks.

"If it did, it didn't last very long," I says.

I don't know if that gives her any comfort.

# 16

I go back into the lobby.

Evergreen's standing there. She's found the time to get dressed, and she's wearing the skirt and blouse to her suit with a sweater thrown over her shoulders.

"Where have you been?" she asks, frowning at me. "You weren't in Mr. Delvin's room."

"I saw he was all right, and then I had a call of nature."

"Oh," she says, as though she don't believe me.

I see Jack Boxer standing by, and Mrs. Child is sitting in the living room staring at her hands.

A police car pulls up at the curb, scraping tire. They ain't sounding their siren, which is a wonder.

I go out on the porch with Evergreen and Boxer behind me. The two uniforms are already past us, cutting across the lawn without even bothering with the paths, their flashlights spraying back and forth, talking to each other in regular voices that sound like they're shouting in the morning quiet. Saying things like, "Did she say in the back of the yard?" and "Maybe we should go up to the door first," and "Is that somebody hiding under that tree?"

Evergreen says, "You stay put, Boxer," and she follows me down the steps and across the lawn in the path of the officers.

They're halfway to the pond when St. John gets up off the bench where he was sitting, almost invisible against the background of the bushes and trees.

"Hey!" one of the cops yells. They both go into a crouch, and one of them draws his gun.

"Jeee-sus!" Robert says, tossing his hands out to the side, able to see them better than they can see him.

"Watch it, Wiley!" the younger cop yells, "he's got a gun."

"I got no gun! I got no gun!" Robert screams. "It be jus' a stick."

"He works here!" I yell, and "Don't shoot!" Evergreen shouts at the same time.

The two cops spin around, and the one with his gun out throws down on me.

Evergreen hurries past me saying, "Here. Here. I'm the one who called."

Wiley straightens up and waits for her to get to him. The other one walks toward me with the beam of the flashlight right in my eyes and the muzzle of the gun pointed at my belly.

"This the cause of the disturbance?" he asks.

I make a gesture as I start to tell him there ain't no disturbance and that the reason for calling the police is lying over by the pond with his nose in the water.

"Don't make any sudden moves, please, sir," the cop says.

"I'm the one found the body," I says.

"We'll talk about that in a minute. Who did you say was that man over there?"

"He's an employee. His name is Robert St. John," Evergreen says.

"Jerry," the cop standing alongside Evergreen says, "there's a dead person lying on the ground over here."

"If you'll just go ahead of me, sir," Jerry says.

I'm not going to stand there arguing about how I'm not the one who put the body there even if he's acting like I could be. We go over to join Evergreen and Wiley, who're already standing with St. John over by the body.

She starts acting very crisp and efficient like she usually acts.

"This is Mr. Flannery, officers. He discovered Mr. Custer and alerted us to the tragedy."

"How's that, Mr. Flannery?" Jerry says, taking a look at Alfie, who's standing by my leg. "You live in the neighborhood?"

"I live over in the Twenty-Seventh on Polk Street."

"That's a long walk, ain't it?"

"That's my car at the curb. I wasn't out taking a stroll."

"What was you out doing?"

"I got a phone call from a friend of mine who's a patient here, and it worried me. So I came to have a look."

"What did he say that worried you?"

"That's just it. He just mumbled some sort of jumble, but I thought it was him, and I thought he could be in trouble."

"Is he in trouble?"

"No, he don't seem to be in trouble. He seems to be sleeping pretty peaceful last time I looked."

"So it wasn't him on the telephone?"

"Probably not."

"So who was it, if it wasn't your friend?"

"I don't know."

"If you came over here to see if your friend was in trouble, how come you found the body way out back?"

I point to Alfie.

"My dog must've heard the ducks and ran back here to have a look."

Alfie gives me a look like he's asking me how come I'm dragging him into this mess. I figure later I'll give him a doggie treat and explain to him that it's better if it looks like I found Mr. Custer when I was chasing after my dog than if I was just nosing around.

"You see anybody else in the area?" Jerry asks me.

"Nobody," I says.

"So that means nobody saw you either," he says, like he's still very suspicious that I'm the one who killed the old man and all the rest of my story is just made up.

"That figures," I says.

"And that means there's nobody can back up your story how your dog ran away to bite a duck and you found the dead man when you went after him."

"I'd say that covers the facts pretty good."

"And then you—"

"Jerry," the other cop—who I can see is ten years older, ten years smarter, and ten years wearier—says, "save the questions."

"I just thought I'd get this investigation rolling, Wiley."

"This investigation is going to get rolling," Wiley says, "when the detectives get here, and the coroner's man gets here, and the mobile forensic lab gets here, and the morgue wagon gets here. Any questions you ask these people, the detectives are going to ask them all over again, and I don't feel like listening to cabbage being chewed twice."

"All right," Jerry says. "Just stay where you are, everybody," he adds, just to show us he ain't lost it altogether.

Two more cars pull up at the curb, one after the other, the first a plain black Plymouth sedan, the second another squad car.

"Get some lights over here," I hear somebody say. "Tape off the area."

"There's nobody on the streets, Sergeant," another voice says.

"So, before you know it, there'll be a crowd. Tape it off."

Two men in plain clothes come across the lawn toward us. I know who they are from their shapes a long time before I see their faces.

One of them is Murray Rourke, a sweet, gentle-acting detective from Special Crimes Squad who, while interrogating a suspect, can change in a watch tick into the scariest monster you ever seen. The other one is Francis O'Shea, who's a scary monster all the time.

"Ah, Jesus, I might of known," O'Shea says the minute he sees me. "If there's a dead body found anywhere in Chicago at some ungodly hour of the night or morning, Flannery's bound to be somewhere nearby."

"Good morning, O'Shea," I says.

"Don't good-morning me. Why did you do it?"

"How are you, Jimmy?" Rourke says. "O'Shea'll have his little joke."

"I have a feeling it's not so much a joke as a wish from his mouth to God's ear," I says.

"Don't you believe it," Rourke says. "He loves you like a brother. It's just hard for him to show it."

O'Shea is squatting down looking Mr. Custer over from about
six feet away. "I see that you trampled all over the joint as usual,
Flannery," he says, looking up at me over his shoulder.

"I walked straight up to him and checked his pulse to see if he
was as dead as he looked," I says. "I couldn't very well let him lie
there without knowing, could I?"

"What about all these other footprints?"

He's pointing here and there on the soft ground.

"One set'll be Mr. Custer's—"

"Who?"

"The man you're looking at."

"How about these others?"

"I ain't got a clue," I says, eyeing these huge footprints going
around the pond and into the bushes that I would've swore wasn't
there when I found the body.

"Mr. Flannery warned us about getting too close when we went
to look at Mr. Custer," Evergreen says. "None of us ever got closer
than you are right now."

She tosses me a look that says she hopes I appreciate how she's
coming to my defense and also giving me a compliment.

O'Shea straightens up. "Well, that's good," he says grudgingly.

"Aren't you going to take him out of the water?" Evergreen
asks.

"We'd like to," Rourke says in his soothing voice, "but we can't
do that until the coroner comes to make his examination."

"Disgraceful," Evergreen says, and she takes a couple of steps
back as the uniforms from the other squad car come over with
some portable floods that they set up to light the scene.

It's getting worse and worse. Any dignity Mr. Custer might've
hoped for in his last hour is being stripped away. Pretty soon the
night watch from the newspaper and stringers for the local
television stations could be coming around asking questions and
taking pictures. Somehow we make a circus out of just about
everything, even when we're trying to do the right thing.

# 17

Before the coroner's man gets there O'Shea herds us all into the house.

Alfie plays it smart and finds a place to lie down out of the traffic.

All the noise must've woke up some of the patients, or maybe five o'clock was the time a couple of them usually get up, because there's two old men and an old woman in her bare feet wandering around asking for their breakfast.

"You got another two hours at least before you can have your breakfast," Jack Boxer says.

Mrs. Spencer, wearing a bathrobe or dressing gown even tattier than the one she lent to Custer, comes shuffling down the hallway into the living room.

"Jack, see what you can do about getting Mr. Barnaby and Mr. Herkimer back to their rooms," Evergreen says, turning her back on the rest of us and hurrying over to the skinny old woman. "What are you doing up so early, Agnes?"

"Couldn't sleep. All the commotion out in the yard."

Evergreen puts her arm around Mrs. Spencer's waist and starts turning her around. "Mrs. Child, will you see that Mrs. Muldoon gets back to her room? And get her into some slippers."

Mrs. Child's already over there taking the other old lady in hand. She's got a pair of unlaced shoes she took from the box in the hallway and kneels down to slip them on Mrs. Muldoon's feet.

"Can I have a streusel bun?" Mrs. Muldoon asks.

"If we have any," Evergreen says. "And Mrs. Child, will you ask Robert to come out and watch the desk?"

"If that sonofabitch, Charlie Custer, ain't et them all, you mean," Mrs. Muldoon says, getting really upset.

"What?" O'Shea says.

"Charlie Custer eats all the streusel buns," Mrs. Muldoon says, really irritated with everybody.

"We'll keep an eye on him and see he doesn't," Evergreen says, letting go of Mrs. Spencer and going to Mrs. Muldoon.

"Hold it," O'Shea says. "Just a second there."

Mrs. Muldoon practically cowers behind Evergreen when she sees this red-faced hulk barreling over toward her.

"How come Charlie Custer eats all the streusel buns?" O'Shea demands.

"Because he creeps out first thing in the morning, after the bakery delivers and before anybody else is even out of bed, and gobbles them all down."

"Was you on the lookout for him this morning?"

"I'm on the lookout for him every morning."

"So you saw him this morning?"

"I didn't say that," she says getting a whiff that something's not so good with Charlie Custer and she better find out what's what before she answers any more questions. She pulls her robe closer around her neck, grabbing hold of her courage and her dignity and says, "Just who in the hell are you?"

"I'm the police."

"What's the police doing running around a respectable neighborhood this time of night?"

"There's been an accident, Mrs. Muldoon," Evergreen says. "Mr. Custer had an accident and died."

"Ever since Hizzoner, Mayor Daley, passed away, the town's been going to hell in a wheelbarrow," Mrs. Muldoon says.

"Your room have a view of the garden?" Rourke asks in his Irish tenor's voice, as soft and sweet as a lover's kiss.

Mrs. Muldoon reacts favorably to that. She simpers and preens a little bit.

"It does."

"And what the good sergeant's asking you, ma'am, is did something wake you up before all these police arrived and woke up the neighborhood?"

"No, Captain, it was the cars and slamming doors that woke me up. And then the lights out in the garden."

"Thank you, dear," Rourke says, "but I'm not a captain."

She tosses a sidelong glance at O'Shea and says, "Well, if you ain't, you should be."

Evergreen starts moving Mrs. Muldoon out of the room, picking up Mrs. Spencer by the elbow on the way.

Rourke takes O'Shea by the arm and moves him off for another private conference.

Just then Robert St. John walks into the room, and everybody looks at him like he's some kind of celebrity.

"Will you take Mrs. Muldoon and Mrs. Spencer to their rooms?" Evergreen says.

I look at St. John's feet. He's got his running shoes laced up now. They're like boats. Must be thirteens, fourteens. Good-looking Reeboks, red, yellow and purple, making them look even bigger than they are. I'm wondering what he was doing walking around the pond and into the bushes when we left him to watch the body.

"Would you mind telling me who you are, sir?" Rourke says in his sweetest voice.

"Ma name is Robert St. John," the Trinidadian says, pronouncing his last name Sinjin.

"You take the lady to her room but you come right back, if you please. Right back, you understand what I'm saying?"

Before St. John can answer, Rourke turns to Evergreen and says, "Have you got a phone I can use?"

"There's one in my office," she says, pointing across the entrance to the door with the sign that says "Director" on it.

"I'll just be a minute," Rourke says, and he goes to make his call.

I can't help wondering who he's going to call. He ain't got a wife or a live-in girl friend, as far as I know.

"What's this about Mr. Custer stealing streusel buns?" I says to Evergreen.

"That's one of the reasons why we've been locking him in nights and even letting him out days only with supervision."

"So how did he get out there by the pond?"

She looks at me like she's wondering the same thing and shrugs her shoulders.

# 18

By the time Rourke's finished with his phone call, Jack Boxer, Mrs. Child, and Robert St. John are all back from putting their charges in their rooms.

Everybody's standing around like the bunch of ducks outside.

A uniform comes in and tells O'Shea something.

O'Shea says, "Okay. Ask them to come here and report when they're done."

Rourke comes out of Evergreen's office and gives O'Shea half a nod.

"Take a seat and rest your feet," O'Shea tells us.

St. John's the last to sit down, crossing his legs and leaning back in the chair. Then he sees Rourke and O'Shea both staring at his feet again, and he straightens up and puts them flat on the floor.

Mrs. Child's sitting on the edge of her chair, her feet tucked back like she's ready to get up and run first chance she gets.

I take the chair closest to the door.

Boxer's sitting on the other side of the doorway.

Evergreen's sitting between me and St. John.

Rourke finds a straight-backed chair and sits down in front of Mrs. Child.

O'Shea stays standing, like a buffalo ready to charge.

"Will you please tell us your name?" Rourke asks Mrs. Child in that nice soft voice he's got.

"Maybelle Child, but everybody calls me May."

"I think I'll call you Mrs. Child. Is that all right with you?"

She loves him already. She's used to people half her age and with a quarter of her experience calling her May on first meeting. Night nurse or no night nurse, she's one of the serving class, and probably everybody treats her in a familiar way.

"Mrs. Child, are you a registered nurse?"

"No sir, but I'm a certified nurse's aide and physician's attendant."

"How long have you been working here at Larkspur?"

"Twenty-seven months."

"Is it a good place to work?"

She hesitates just a flicker, her eyes darting to Evergreen. "It's fine."

It was only a flutter, but I caught it, and I'm pretty sure Rourke and O'Shea caught it, too.

I'm surprised when O'Shea don't lean in and start bullying her a little, scaring her a little bit. Maybe he's getting smarter in his old age. Maybe I don't know him as good as I think I do.

"Do you always work last out?" O'Shea asks.

"Pardon?" Mrs. Child says, her eyebrows going up to show she don't understand the question.

"My partner means do you always work the midnight-to-eight shift?" Rourke says.

"I've been working it the last four months."

"Why's that?" Rourke asks.

"Pardon?" she says again, but this time there's no eyebrows. She understands the question and what he's getting at.

"I'm trying to figure out the organization here. Does personnel rotate shifts like they do in hospitals? Do people volunteer for night work? How's it work?"

She shakes her head to the questions.

"Did you volunteer for night work?"

She hesitates again even though she wants to please him. I can tell she's a person who hates to lie, but there's obviously other things she's considering—like keeping her job—and she's lying. Her eyes flicker to Evergreen again.

"The night shift is usually given to the newest qualified probationer," Evergreen says.

"Why's that?" Rourke asks. "It seems to me that supervising the whole facility all alone, at night, is a pretty heavy responsibility."

"There's not a lot to do. If an emergency comes up, and the night attendant hasn't had sufficient experience to handle it, there's always an experienced person in the on-call room. If they need instruction, there's always me. I live here."

O'Shea looks at St. John. "You were in the on-call room tonight?"

"That's right."

Mrs. Spencer told me St. John was supposed to be on the desk. Somebody's telling a couple of lies here or the old lady's got it wrong, which at her age is expected.

"Mrs. Child, you've been employed here two years and three months," Rourke goes on. "Surely there have been people hired after you. Yet you tell me that you've been on nights for four months?"

May looks at Evergreen every time a question's asked, but Evergreen won't meet her eye. She's looking at the corner of the room, her mind going a mile a minute, trying to work something out.

"Well, actually I was on call tonight, and Mr. St. John was on duty," Mrs. Child finally says.

St. John and Evergreen both look at her like she just let a cat out of the bag.

"Oh, how come you were at the desk, then?" O'Shea asks.

Mrs. Child hesitates. She knows she let the cat out and now she's sorry, but she don't know how to put it back. "He said he needed some personal time," she stammers.

A blush rises up Evergreen's neck and all over her face like she's got a fever.

I'm thinking about the stockings and the garter belt and St. John's unlaced running shoes.

"How much personal time?" Rourke asks pleasantly.

"I don't know," Mrs. Child says, making it sound like she can't pin it down because it wasn't really all that much.

But O'Shea's right on top of her. "How much?" he asks in a voice that would scare a gorilla.

"He said an hour, maybe two hours," Mrs. Child says, ready to bust out into tears.

"Did that make you a little upset? I mean Mr. St. John asking you to take part of his shift for him when you've been working nights all this time and could have been having your rest in the on-call room?" Rourke asks in this very sympathetic way.

"I didn't mind doing him the favor," she says, but you don't have to be a mental giant to see she minded a lot.

"He call you from the desk and ask you to relieve him?"

"That's right."

"Were you in bed?"

"Yes."

"And did you get right up and get dressed and go take over the watch?"

She don't answer right away.

"Ma'am," Rourke says very kindly, "was Mr. St. John waiting at the desk when you finally got there?"

"Finally?" she says, like this was a dangerous word.

"Well, I just mean I suppose it would've taken you ten, fifteen minutes to get dressed and comb your hair and walk down the hall from the on-call room."

She sits there staring at him.

"It take you longer than fifteen minutes, Mrs. Child?"

"Maybe a little longer," she says.

"Maybe as much as half an hour, forty minutes?"

"Maybe."

He straightens up and turns his head to look at St. John like it was a very brutal and unfair thing to do, asking this poor woman to leave her bed and take over his night watch. Then he looks at Mrs. Child again and says, "And was Mr. St. John still at the desk when you got there?"

You can tell that now she realizes that Rourke got her feeling so sorry for herself for being put upon by St. John, the island charmer, that she blew the whistle on him. You can tell that now she feels like she betrayed him to the enemy.

"No," she says, in a little voice nobody can hardly hear.

Rourke turns around so he's facing St. John head on. O'Shea turns his body and sways forward so his face is practically in St. John's face.

"Is that right, Mr. St. John?" Rourke asks.

St. John's looking at Evergreen like he expects her to get him out of the soup.

Rourke don't follow up right away. Like he wants to give St. John some time to think it out. He looks at Evergreen, too. "I could really use a cup of coffee," he says, smiling sweetly.

"I ordered the kitchen helper to brew up early," Evergreen says. "I told her to bring some in here as soon as it's ready. Do you want me to go see about it?"

"No, no. I can wait. Thank you for the thought."

Rourke's all of a sudden throwing charm around by the bucketful. I'm getting the picture of the way a mongoose sort of circles around the cobra, tiptoeing here and there, sniffing at everything but the snake, giving him the old one-eye, waiting for the opening, the psychological moment.

"You ain't answered the question," O'Shea says. He's the bad cop. He don't have to be subtle. All he's got to do is scare the hell out of the person under interrogation and scare him into Rourke's arms.

"I lef' before Miz Child come," St. John says.

"You couldn't take this *personal* time you needed after Mrs. Child relieved you?"

"Well . . ."

"You had to take it right then and there? What was so important you had to take this *personal* time right then and there, that second?"

St. John's face tightens up, and you can see he's thinking about turning himself into a stone.

There's the sound of something squeaking coming down the hallway, and a minute later a young woman in a white kitchen smock and cap comes wheeling in a cart with a towel draped over the top shelf. There's a big aluminum pitcher with steam coming out of it. A quart container of half and half, a box of sugar cubes, and some plastic spoons. Nothing fancy. No china. No silverware. A no-frills cup of coffee for the intruders.

Evergreen waves the kitchen help away and pours coffee into thick white mugs herself. I get up and hand them all around, O'Shea taking one for hisself and one for Rourke. St. John, Mrs. Child, Boxer, and me take one. Evergreen don't pour one for herself.

Rourke's acting like he's at a tea party, his legs crossed, elbow on his knee, holding up the mug and taking a delicate sip.

O'Shea's still threatening St. John with his ape grin.

St. John's leaning forward, putting some half and half into his mug of coffee, probably hoping the interruption will make the questions go away.

"What kind of personal time were you taking for an hour or two, St. John?" Rourke asks him, like they was old friends chatting about things that didn't matter.

"Well, like Mrs. Child say, it be personal."

"That's a wise guy's answer, you know what I mean?" O'Shea says.

"You left your post unattended, Robert," Rourke says. "Anybody wants to, they could charge you with dereliction of duty. Maybe *criminal* dereliction of duty. That could be a class C felony. Pull some time."

St. John looks at Evergreen with that look again, asking for a little help.

Evergreen clears her throat like a nervous poker player ready to plunge and go for broke.

"I asked Mr. St. John to attend to something for me," she says.

The way she says it, nobody, not even O'Shea, asks her what.

# 19

It ain't long before Harold Boardman, the man from Forensics, comes in with Artie Margolis, the coroner's man. They're finished examining Mr. Custer.

O'Shea and Rourke go over, and they all get their heads together for a little conference.

I can't hear it all, but I'm on the eary and I can get some of it.

". . . photographs of the man's head in the water?" O'Shea asks.

The two experts give each other a look like they're saying, "What the hell is the flatfoot asking stupid questions for?" They don't even answer him but just grunt like they figure he understands monkey talk.

". . . casts . . . footprints," Rourke says, in his softer voice.

They nod their heads, respecting Rourke a little more, but still not giving him any conversation.

". . . struggle?" Rourke asks.

Boardman finally says something, but I can't hear him. All I can tell is he's saying Mr. Custer had signs of a blow right at the temple on the right-hand side. Which he could get from falling down as well as other ways.

". . . very old man," Margolis says. "Very, very old."

I start wandering over, hoping I can catch some longer tail ends. O'Shea sees me coming, frowns, and waves me off.

Boardman looks at me and says, "How's it going, Jimmy?"

"I don't know, Harold. Hanging in."

Margolis looks at me and gives me the nod.

O'Shea gives up waving me off and just looks disgusted.

"I guess you can go take the old man's nose out of the water," Rourke says, at the same time O'Shea says to me, "Get your nose out of this, Flannery. There's nothing to interest you here."

"What do you mean?"

Boardman and Margolis, ready to go, raise their hands like we're all lodge brothers. Boardman notices he's still wearing a rubber glove and quickly strips it off like he's done something rude at the dinner table.

"We'll know more after the autopsy," Boardman says.

"But I'm willing to bet it'll show up death by drowning," Margolis adds.

"Death by misadventure," Boardman says, and then they walk out together, anxious to finish up and go somewhere to have breakfast.

O'Shea's about to tell me what he means in no uncertain terms, but Rourke puts his arm around my shoulders and keeps me there like I'm one of the boys. So we're standing there like three pals.

"You know what we think, Jimmy?" Rourke says.

"What do you think?" I says.

"We think the old man got up and went wandering around on his own."

"Got past the night nurse somehow," O'Shea chips in.

"Got disoriented and confused the way old people get, you know what I mean?" Rourke says.

"Stumbled and fell down. Maybe hit his head on a stone by the side of the pond," O'Shea says, like he's the second half of the vaudeville act.

"Had a heart attack maybe," Rourke says. "They could find out he had a heart attack—a man his age—when they do the P.M. Fell on the ground, his nose in the water."

"Very sad. A man drowns in three inches of water at the side of a pond."

"Happens every day," Rourke says.

"What we're saying here, Flannery," O'Shea says, putting the screw on it, "is that we don't want anybody yelling murder and mayhem when it's probably only misadventure," Rourke says.

"The least we got here is criminal neglect," I says.

"Maybe we got that," O'Shea says, "but that ain't our department."

"Wrongful death ain't your department?"

"Now you're talking like a lawyer, fachrissake, Flannery," O'Shea complains.

"Listen, Jimmy—" Rourke starts to say, but O'Shea cuts him off.

"Put it another way," O'Shea says, doing his baboon threat display imitation. "We don't want you yelling murder where there ain't no murder. We know you work in the sewers, but we don't want you throwing no shit in the fan."

# 20

Rourke and O'Shea go back to the others to tell them this and that.

I run upstairs and look in on Delvin. Alfie gets up from where he's been laying down and trots after me.

Delvin's still asleep, looking gray as a bone and all wrung out, so I don't even try to wake him. I just stand there feeling a little sick from the sour smell in the room, and then I go to Agnes Spencer's room.

I'm just about to knock on the door when Jack Boxer appears at the end of the hall, walking toward me with the look of a guy what's ready to scramble.

"What're you doing here?" I says.

"That's what they asked me to find out about you," Boxer says, grinning this shark's grin at me.

"Who asked you to find out?"

"Your cop friends. They wanted to say good-bye."

"They still downstairs?"

"They couldn't wait. They told me to remind you not to throw anything at the fan. So what are you doing hanging around the old lady's room?"

"What old lady? I was just looking in on my friend one more time before I go home."

"That ain't your friend's room."

I look up and down the corridor like I'm confused.

"Come on," he says, "I'll show you the way back to the parlor. You don't really want to bother your friend. He ain't had his breakfast yet."

What can I do? I go along.

I walk down the hallway with Boxer dogging me.

Downstairs, the only person around is Mrs. Child, sitting at the desk like she's ready to pay with extra effort for letting the cat out of the bag about Evergreen and St. John.

I ask can I use the telephone on the desk, and she tells me it's only an inside phone and you can't call out on it. I ask if Evergreen's in her office. She says she ain't, that she went outside to watch them take Mr. Custer away and she ain't come back.

"Why don't you get the hell outta here?" Boxer growls at me. "You need a phone, go find a gas station, go find a drug store."

I take a handful of change out of my pocket for the pay phone, which is in an alcove near the door to the sun porch, and start poking through it. I don't even bother looking at him. I just say, "Listen, you, go find something to do. If you'd rather duke it out with me, that's okay, too. But I got to tell you, I don't fight fair. Give me the chance and I'll bust your kneecap, take out your eye."

Alfie looks up at him and growls, showing a little tooth, backing me up.

I find the coin I need, and then I look at Boxer.

He swooshes through his nose like he don't think much of my threats but ain't got the time to put them to the test. But I think he also sees I mean it, so he walks away, squeaking down the tiles in his sneakers.

I call Mary at Passavant to tell her what I found when I got over to Larkspur that morning.

"Don't jump to any conclusions, James," she says. "Old people get up in the night and don't know where they are. They wander off and get themselves into difficulty. A lot of times they're on medication, which adds to the disorientation of people suffering the onslaught of senility. Not every death is a murder. Just remember that."

"I won't go looking for trouble," I says, "but I smell something rotten around this place, and I'm going to try to figure out what it is before old Delvin gets hurt by it some way."

"If you want to take him out of there today, Jimmy, we can always put him up with us. We can get a hospital bed. We can make do."

I tell her that I can't get him out of the nursing home at the moment anyway because this distant relative, Carmody, has got hisself a guardianship and ain't about to make it easy for me.

"Be careful, James," she says, starting to smell something rotten, too, even though she's on the other side of town.

I hang up and go over to Mrs. Child. "They take away the coffee cart?"

She nods. "There's coffee in the dining room."

"I'm going to get myself a cup. You want me to bring you a cup?"

She's in need of kindness. She nods her head and puts a handkerchief up to her nose.

"Cream and sugar?"

"If you please," she says.

I go into the dining room. There's some patients and staff in there having breakfast. They all look at me like I could have the answers to all the questions they'd like to ask.

Mrs. Muldoon is stuffing streusel buns into her mouth because on this unusual day there's nobody says she can't. I go over and ask her can I have a little bite of one of her buns for my dog. She gives me half a bun, but she ain't happy about it.

I take the coffee and the half a bun back to the front desk.

Alfie takes the treat from me like it's about time I give a little thought to his welfare. I lay the mugs down on the desk and pull up a straight-backed chair.

Mrs. Child and me both take a swallow, looking over the rims of the mugs at each other like we're old friends sharing hard times.

"The cops shouldn't have tricked you into telling on Robert," I says.

"Well, you want to know, I warned Robert not to be a fool."

"A fool about what?"

"About that woman."

"What woman?"

"Miz Evergreen."

"I don't get your meaning."

"She's got the power over men."

I almost bust out laughing. Garter belt or no garter belt I can't imagine chunky little Lenore Evergreen doing no vampire act, putting somebody like St. John under a spell. I can understand that maybe St. John is taking advantage of her, loving her up for some privileges and maybe job security, but if anybody's being used in the relationship it's her, not him.

"You don't believe me," Mrs. Child says. "That's part of her power. She can turn it on and off like a faucet."

"You saying she's the cause of what's wrong around here?"

"Like the quality of the food going down and down? Like there not being enough staff to take care of the patients so sometimes some of these old people is tied down in their beds with restraints because it's easier to manage them that way when you ain't got enough supervision? Like rats in the basement and cockroaches in the kitchen and bedbugs in the beds because the exterminators don't come and the sheets don't get washed as much as they should?"

"This place's had a lot of black marks against it for a lot longer than Evergreen's been here."

"Oh, that's so. But it's been getting worse since she took over."

"Well, Ms. Evergreen's new to the job."

"All you got to have is eyes to see."

"You file any complaints?"

"That's why I've been working nights for four months. I complained."

"That would've been before Ms. Evergreen took over?"

"Mr. Betancourt was still here, but she was already taking over," Mrs. Child says. "But that ain't all, that ain't all."

"What else?"

All of a sudden she looks scared, like she's said more than she meant to say.

I take her hands. "Hey, you got to share your worries and your troubles. I'm not a cop. I'm not a city official. I'm just somebody with a friend in this place, and I'd like to keep him safe. You think somebody's skimming the operating budget? You think somebody's trying to get rich on poor service?"

"I don't know. I don't know," she kind of moans. "If it was only that."

"Something worse than that?"

"Mr. Custer ain't the first old person to die in a funny way."

"It's happened before?"

"That's what I'm saying."

"Recently?"

"Four months ago, and a month before that. First the husband, then the wife. Mr. and Mrs. Felton. William and Lucy Felton."

The short hairs on the back of my neck and the backs of my hands are tingling.

"Were the police called in?"

"No, sir. They said the old people died natural deaths, and they was buried, and that was that."

"You know where Ms. Evergreen went?" I asks, standing up.

"You're not going to tell her what I said?" Mrs. Child says, scared all over again.

"I might have to ask the question, but I won't say where I got the idea."

I took another swallow of coffee just because it was hot.

"This is really bad coffee," I says.

"Dishwater," she says, and somehow that makes us both smile.

Evergreen's out by the duck pond, just like Mrs. Child said she was, standing well back, looking at the outline chalked on the grass and stone border. The ducks're waddling around in circles, complaining about how somebody took their picnic away. Or maybe they're just doing what ducks do all the time.

She shivers when I come up behind her even though the sun's up and warming the air by now.

"I may have to get rid of those ducks," she says. "Every time I look at them from now on I won't see funny fat things, I'll see monsters that were feeding on poor old Mr. Custer."

I'm thinking about how I can approach the subject of the Feltons without putting the finger on Mrs. Child.

Evergreen turns around and faces me. She takes a step closer to me so she's got to look up at me even though I ain't very tall. I don't know what she's done, but all of a sudden she don't look square and stocky, she looks soft and round. Her hair's loose and blowing around her face and neck in the morning breeze. She's unbuttoned her blouse, and I can see the tops of breasts swelling up, as white as two scoops of vanilla ice cream. "Should I interpret your silence as disapproval?" she asks.

"What?"

"Chicago Irish. As prejudiced a bunch as you'll find anywhere." The way she says it, it's a challenge, but it ain't an insult.

"Oh?" I says.

"'Oh?' What does that mean?"

"It means I'm surprised you come out with what was going on just like that."

She tilts her head and blinks her eyes very slow. She wets her lips, her pink tongue flicking out in slow motion. I can tell she's laughing at me a little.

"Catholic Irish to boot," she says. "Sex and sin. Sex and sin. Especially with a nigger." She puts a drop of acid in the last crack.

I'm beginning to think Mrs. Child could be right. I don't know what's happening, but the way Evergreen's looking at me I feel like she's putting her hands on me.

"I don't like that word."

"Sex, sin, or nigger?" she asks me and laughs.

"I don't even like it when black people use it about themselves."

"Are you a saintly man, Jimmy?" she says, and she puts her hand on my wrist. It's like a spark goes through me, like the trick my old man used to pull on me when I was a kid and he'd shuffle along the rug, picking up static, and point his finger at my nose so a spark would snap. "Are you ready to forgive me my sins?"

"I'm just trying to tell you it never entered my mind should you, shouldn't you go to bed with Robert St. John or anybody else you want to go to bed with, though I don't know how smart it is for a boss to go to bed with an employee, if you really want to know what I think."

She turns her head. She lifts one hand and pulls her hair away from her face. She closes the neck of her blouse with the other. She slouches, and all of a sudden she's chunky little Lenore Evergreen again.

"Everyone's so quick to jump to conclusions, aren't they?" she says. "I never said I slept with Robert. All I said was that I asked him to attend to something for me."

She looks at me like she just won a business negotiation. I can see she's got a low opinion of me and my intelligence.

She turns away from me like she's dismissing me.

"You want to tell me how Mr. and Mrs. Felton died?" I says to her back.

# 21

Who told you about Mr. and Mrs. Felton?" Evergreen asks me when we're sitting on the bench under the willow tree with the ducks making soft quack-quack conversation.

"That don't matter, does it?" I says. "I don't want to light any fires under any pots."

"The Feltons died during the transition period. I hadn't completely taken charge yet," she says.

Her voice is ordinary. There's no music in it.

"Who was in charge?"

"I'm not ducking any blame."

It's like I already forget what it felt like when she was looking up at me with her head tilted to one side.

"I didn't say you was."

"Mr. Betancourt. He's been promoted to the board of the corporation that runs Larkspur and the other facilities."

She's got her hair pinned back in a bun again. I hardly saw her do it.

"How many more nursing homes have they got?"

"Thirty-two or -three of them, scattered over seven states."

"So this Betancourt gets hisself out of management and kicked upstairs right after these two people die?"

"I don't know what you've been told, but there was never any question of deliberate wrongdoing. They were accidents."

"Two people die, especially two related people, and you got to think it could be more than accidents. Which one died first?"

"Mr. Felton. He was left momentarily unattended in the bath. He apparently slipped under the water and drowned."

"Nobody heard him thrashing around? He didn't yell out?"

"He may have been medicated at the time."

"So an old drugged-out man was left alone in a bathtub. Who was it left him there?"

"I don't know."

"How could that be?"

"No one stepped forward to take responsibility."

"How about the duty roster?"

"It was missing. It never showed up."

"What did the cops have to say about that?"

"They were never called. What good would it have done?"

"The coroner was notified, wasn't he?"

"Oh, yes. The health department was informed as well, according to the law. The death certificate was duly signed."

"Well, signatures and documents ain't that hard to come by."

"You're a very suspicious man, aren't you, Jimmy?" she says. "It was an accident. It shouldn't have happened, but it did, and nothing would have been served if it had been made into more than it was."

"It could've closed this place down."

"That's what I mean, Jimmy. It would have just created more misery and hardship for the people we're trying to care for."

"How about the wife? How did she pass away?"

"There was a mix-up in her medication for a heart condition. Too much was administered and brought on an attack instead of preventing one."

"You telling me this medicine was just lying around, or that she was medicating herself?"

"Medicines are delivered by the dose. No one knew how she'd gotten hold of the bottle. It might even have been empty when she found it."

"What do you mean?"

"The old lady may have saved up the pills and put them in an empty bottle she'd found."

"How'd she save up a bottle of pills?"

"It would have been easy enough for her to conceal the pills under her tongue and pretend to wash them down with sips of water, then spit them out in a napkin when the attendant's back was turned."

"Save them up with the idea of taking her own life?"

"That might have been the case. She was very depressed after her husband's death."

"Was there any investigation into her death?"

"There seemed no reason at the time. After all, she had a heart condition and died of a heart attack. They found the empty bottle only after the death certificate had been signed and she'd been buried."

"She was never autopsied?"

"She wouldn't have been. She died while under the care of a physician."

"Her own doctor?"

"A contract doctor with the corporation."

"Can you get me this doctor's name?"

"His name is Irwin Seltzer."

"You just said there was no investigation at the time. You saying you think there should've been one?"

"No. I'm saying that some very persistent rumors started going around after the empty pill bottle was found. I don't think there should have been an investigation because there was wrongful death but just to put the rumors to rest. They can destroy an establishment and ruin reputations. I'm just saying that I think rumors that persist should be looked into."

"So do I."

"But they finally died down."

"That's the way things do most of the time. But you had another chance to mention them other two incidents to the cops this time around. Why didn't you?"

She looks me square in the eye.

"I made a call to Mr. Betancourt the moment Mrs. Child came to me with the news that a man was at the door claiming to have found a body back at the pond."

"Even before you saw for yourself?"

"I wanted to be prepared."

"So what did he say?"

"He advised me to say nothing about the other mishaps."

"Why'd he do that, do you think?"

She looks so bewildered and distressed that for a second I think she's going to cry, but she grabs herself by the scruff of the neck and gives herself a shake.

"To try to keep Larkspur going. It's always under attack. It's easy enough to say things should be better, but nobody does much to make them better. So the rest of us—the ones who care—do the best we can with what we have.

"Larkspur was getting bad reports from the ombudsmen sent out by the citizens' watchdog committee. In fact, Jimmy, I was brought in here to turn this establishment around. Put it back into working order. You think things are pretty bad now. They were in a shambles when I took over three months ago. Morale was low. Revenues were declining. Expenses were going through the roof. The employees were not very good at all, except for one or two like Mrs. Child and Mr. St. John. And Jack Boxer. He's got an attitude problem and a short fuse, but you must believe me, he knows his job and works hard at it.

"I've been making progress. I have to face the accidental death of Mr. Custer, because that occurred on my watch, but I don't know what good would be served by opening up speculation about the Feltons. It would only hinder me in my task."

"It'll also put the corporation under the gun and in line to get sued for a lot of money. Wouldn't the relatives of the Feltons like to know the truth? Haven't they asked any questions?"

"Any questions asked were answered. Apparently there was never any doubt that the deaths were not caused by gross negligence or illegal intent."

"Is that what the relatives say?"

"There's only the one. A niece. Jeannie Felton. She's an extraordinary young woman. Kind and sympathetic. She volunteers to come here whenever she finds the time and does what she can to cheer up our guests."

"Do you mean she works here?"

"She volunteers her time."

"Was she a volunteer when her aunt and uncle died?"

"I believe that she started donating her time and services when they were first admitted and she first came to visit them. Very often that's how volunteers start getting interested."

"Can you give me the name and address of the corporation?" I asks.

"In the office. It's called Fair Winds, Incorporated."

"Where's it headquartered?"

"Right here in Chicago."

We both stand up. She stumbles a little like she's all wore out. I reach out for her, and she puts her hand on my wrist. Only this time there's no spark. It's just the hand of somebody trying to keep from falling.

When we go inside the house, Carmody comes walking out of Evergreen's office.

He looks at me and frowns. "I heard there was an accident," he says to Evergreen.

"Mr. Custer wandered outside in the dark early this morning. It looks like he stumbled down by the duck pond and hit his head."

"Drowned," I says.

He winces. "I'm so sorry to hear that. Everyone else all right? My cousin all right?"

"We was just going to see," I says.

He comes along with us down the hall to Delvin's room.

Evergreen taps on the door very gently. A sweet voice tells us to come in.

I push open the door and walk in first.

Delvin's sitting up in bed with clean pillows piled up behind his back and head. There's a pink cloth napkin tucked into the top of his nightshirt and covering his chest.

A very pretty young woman is feeding him from a bowl of hot cereal. She turns her head and smiles at us.

If I was a teenager, I'd be in love. She's got this sweet round face and soft blond hair framing it, blue eyes, and pink lips. She looks like one of them porcelain figures holding a lamb in its arms.

"Mr. Flannery, Jeannie Felton. Ms. Felton, James Flannery, a friend of Mr. Delvin's," Evergreen says like she's just pulled off a magic trick by producing the young woman we was talking about.

Jeannie Felton is looking at Carmody.

"Oh, I'm sorry," Evergreen said. "I thought you two knew each other."

"I've seen Ms. Felton once or twice," Carmody says, "but we've never been introduced."

"Mr. Francis Carmody, Ms. Jeannie Felton," Evergreen says.

Delvin is looking at us like he's happy to have a crowd. But when he looks at me I can see he don't even know who I am. I could cry.

My old Chinaman's aged a hundred years. He's lost so much weight that there's no flesh on his cheeks, and his false teeth look like the teeth of an old horse.

I got to ask him twice how he's feeling before he finally smiles and says, "Pretty good, Pop."

# 22

While we're sitting down at the supper table I tell Mike and Mary all about William and Lucy Felton and how I find their niece, Jeannie, feeding Delvin with a spoon. Also how it looks like Rourke calls in to find out how to proceed in the death of Mr. Custer, and how I'm suspicious that maybe the deaths of Mr. and Mrs. Felton were stepped on because certain people got an interest in the financial well-being of the Larkspur Nursing Home.

I tell them about the affair going on between the director, Lenore Evergreen, and the Trinidadian orderly, Robert St. John.

Mike winces a little, but he don't say anything about that.

I tell them how Mr. Custer was found wearing Mrs. Spencer's robe because they'd taken his clothes away and locked him in his room. And I tell them how I'd asked Mr. Custer for the location of Delvin's room, and how I'd made up that I was investigating things around the Larkspur and he could help me.

"Why'd you do that?" Mike asks.

"He looked like a man who needed something to do, you know what I mean? I thought I was doing him a kindness."

"Like giving a kid something to do on a rainy Sunday afternoon?" Mike says, making it sound like I was looking down on the old man.

"It was dumb," I says.

He don't say it wasn't dumb even though Mary puts her hand

on mine to let me know she understands I was trying to do something nice.

"I keep on wondering if maybe he was on the lookout because I asked him to be and saw something he wasn't supposed to see."

"For God's sake," Mike says, "don't go gathering up a sack of guilty feelings."

I tell them about Mrs. Muldoon complaining about him eating all the streusel buns and about St. John walking around the pond into the bushes after he was left alone to guard the body.

"Took a pee," Mike says, "excuse the language, Mary. His bladder got full, but he couldn't go inside to use the toilet because he'd been told to watch a corpse."

"I never thought of that."

"Simple explanations are usually the best. What are you doing? You looking for mayhem because an old woman told you Custer ate all the streusel buns or because he had to borrow another old woman's bathrobe or a guy from Trinidad got took short?"

"I didn't say none of it meant anything. I was just bouncing it off you."

"Well, I think you're imagining the worst because you're worried about Delvin. But it sounds to me like the old man's doing better at that nursing home than he'd be doing at his own house all alone."

"He thought I was his father. He called me Pop."

"He was having his little joke. He was pulling your leg in front of the pretty girl."

"I know you're making jokes so I shouldn't start brooding about maybe there's something dirty in Denmark, but—"

"No, I'm making jokes so you shouldn't start sticking your nose in places where it don't belong."

"Three old people up and died in that place under mysterious circumstances."

"One way to look at it. The other way to look at it is one old man fell asleep or maybe passed out and drowned in the bathtub. Maybe some neglect there, even if the attendant only left him alone for a minute or two. Or even less than a minute or two. But that don't make it homicide."

"Nobody took the blame."

"Just because you take the blame and I take the blame for what we do don't mean everybody takes the blame. Where've you been all your life? Don't you know that everybody ducks the blame?"

It's the truth, so all I can do is nod.

"Now the old woman what dies of heart failure. You say there's a rumor she got an overdose of the heart medicine that was supposed to keep it ticking but stopped it instead. But there's nobody around to swear it was an overdose. What you got with heart attacks is you got funny things happening. Chickie Banducci, forty-five years of age, leaves his doctor's office with a clean bill of health and the promise he'll live to be a hundred. Goes to the Sold Out Saloon that night. Has three plates of kielbasa and cabbage. Takes Gertie O'Hara home with him for a slap and a tickle—excuse the vulgarity, Mary—and drops dead while doing a knee bend. Who's to say? Who's to know?"

That's worth another nod.

"And finally you got another old man goes wandering off and falls facedown in a duck pond and drowns. That's what you got."

"Well, when you put it that way."

"So we got to do what we can," Mike says. "I smell dead fish."

"What?" I says.

My old man's got this thing. I say something, and he says the opposite. Sometimes he'll turn me around a little to his way of thinking. Maybe I'll even start agreeing with him. Then, the next thing you know, he'll do a hundred and eighty and argue my case like I was standing up for his.

"Well, Jim, you can't just stand by and see your old Chinaman abused and neglected, lying there all drugged up so he can't even feed himself."

"I wasn't going to stand by—"

"You can't abandon Delvin like he was an old dog."

Alfie sits up and gives me a look like what kind of person am I? Could I be thinking about throwing him out when he starts getting long in the tooth?

"I never—"

"Ah, Jim, is that the way I raised you? Show a little pity. Show a little compassion. Show a little gratitude."

# 23

**M**iles Betancourt. You got to figure with a name like that the man's got to have a pencil-line mustache, hair slicked back and parted in the middle, and the smile of a ticket taker in a carny.

Instead, this Miles Betancourt looks like everybody's idea of a grandfather or favorite uncle, with a walrus mustache—a little yellow at the ends from smoking cigarettes—rough gray hair that looks like he combs it with his fingers, and a smile what could melt your heart.

His shirt's hanging halfway out of his trousers in back, and he keeps working his suspenders like they're bothering his shoulders.

He lights up a cigarette and waves it in the air.

"I promise myself to give it up every night, but I reach for one first thing every morning. You get ahold of a bad habit when you're young, and it's hell giving it up when you're old."

"I know the feeling," I says, just to be polite.

"You're too young to know the feeling, Jim," he says, though behind this old country boy act I figure he's maybe forty-three, forty-four. "Is it all right if I call you Jim?"

"Sure."

"Don't call me Miles, though. The corporation thinks it looks good on the letterhead and the office door, but I think that's because it was my father's name and he was a force to be reckoned with back when."

I don't ask him a force to be reckoned with about what, but I never heard of any heavy players named Betancourt in the political history of Chicago. Which means one of two things. Either the Betancourt family was or is so rich that they worked their politics behind the scenes or so pious they never wanted to put a foot in the door.

"So call me Mick," he goes on.

"My father's name is Mike. Sometimes people call him Mick. The wrong person calls him Mick, he's liable to get a fist in the nose."

"Well, names. Funny thing about names. I wonder sometimes if we become what we become and act like we act because of the names people call us or if people call us this or that because of the way they see us."

"So they see you Irish?"

"I am Irish, Jim. Don't let the Betancourt fool you. There's a lot of Betancourts back in the old country. People emigrated from place to place then just like they do now. Betancourts came from France and settled in Ireland. Did you know that Edgar Allan Poe's family name was originally La Poer?"

"I didn't know that," I says, wondering if Betancourt's trying to make chatty conversation or give me the snoot.

"But you didn't come to talk to me about French or Irish emigration, did you, Jim?"

"No, I didn't. I came to find out something about your business."

"How's that? You want to go into it? Are you thinking about making a career in the health care profession? What is it you're doing now?"

"I'm a sewer inspector for the city."

He makes a little face likes he smells something and then laughs to show me he's only being funny. "I don't blame you, Jim, if I had to inspect sewers all day I'd get away from the smell as quick as I could."

"Is that why you quit managing the Larkspur, Mick? Was the smell getting to you?"

All of a sudden his old country boy drawl takes on a hard edge.

"The smell of old people pissing themselves, do you mean, Jim? The smell of people crapping their pants? The smell of decay and sickness and death. Is that what you're talking about, Jim?"

"Some people would call it the smell of don't-give-a-damn. The smell of neglect."

"The operation looks a little frayed around the edges to you, does it, Jim? Understaffed? Underfunded?"

"I took a look at the prices you charge, so it can't be underfunding."

"You think not? You think the corporation's in there tearing excessive profit out of the hides of old folks?"

"Something ain't right, and you know it," I says, getting a little hot around the collar myself.

That seems to settle him down. He swivels around so he's looking at the wall. I take a look, too. There's a big painting of rolling hills with a dirt road meandering through it, a house on the hill under a spreading oak, and cows dotted all over the meadows.

When he starts talking again his voice is like rough honey. He sounds like I heard Carl Sandburg sound once when he recited some of his poems when I was a kid in grammar school.

"People come into our rest homes suffering from old age and all the pains and ills that go along with it. Their sons or daughters, wives or husbands, nephews, nieces, or cousins take a lot of time to find a place for good old Tom and dear old Nell. Sometimes Tom or Nell have a bit put by. They worked all their lives and think they've been wise and prudent, saving up enough to see them through to the end in reasonable comfort. Or the relatives are willing to help out with whatever they've got.

"But a year goes by, maybe two. Prices go up. The value of money goes down. Pretty soon they're running out of savings. They're holding on to a house or some stocks and bonds, perhaps. Something to leave behind for those who cared.

"Well, they can't keep it, Jim. Oh, no. There's a means test for long-term care. Government welfare can't stand the burden. We vote against the taxes it'd take to pay the costs. So the old people have to impoverish themselves if they want to go welfare all the way.

"Except. Except the nursing homes and convalescence homes can't make it on what the welfare pays them. So pretty soon they got to make the choice. Eat some of the expenses of these indigent old people themselves or kick them out into the street. Maybe somebody'll scoop them up. Maybe not. If they get put into a public facility, it's the next thing to hell.

"Are you listening to what I'm telling you, Jim?"

I'm practically hypnotized. Looking at that painting of the country scene and listening to his warm voice rolling over me, I'm practically asleep. If he wants to sell me an oceangoing yacht for sailing on the lake, I'm ready to plunk my money down. I take my eyes away from the painting and put them back on Betancourt.

"I'm listening, but I ain't sure I'm getting the message."

"The message is we do what we can do. Any shortcomings you may have found out at Larkspur are due to compassion and doing the best we can. That's why I got myself onto the board, Jim. I'm trying to see if there's a way I can turn things around and save these old people from up here, closer to the top."

I'm practically stammering when I ask him could he explain what happened to the Feltons when he was at Larkspur and what happened to Mr. Custer just the other night.

"Lack of staff, Jim. Everybody overworked. Fourteen-, fifteen-hour days. Double shifts without sleep. Too many patients. Lack of funds. It's like you find yourself in a cage just small enough to turn around in, and there's a machine dropping billiard balls on your head. It gets so you're so busy ducking the billiard balls you can't find the time to figure out a way to reach out and turn off the damn machine. You get my meaning, Jim?"

"You still haven't explained what happened to the Feltons. Did they happen to be a couple of the poor ones?"

He looks me full in the face, giving me the old sincerity. Letting me know that he's a little disappointed in what I'm doing. Telling me he knows that what I'm doing is accusing him of maybe putting these old people to sleep like they was old dogs. Read the papers, it's happening every day.

"Do I look like one of these 'Angels of Death'?" he says, like he's reading my mind.

"Do I look like a guy what works down in the sewers?" I says, making a joke out of it.

"Point taken. I wish I could put your heart at rest, Jim. Three accidents happened inside of three months. It might seem like clockwork. It might even seem like a killer's striking during the full moon, like some serial killers are supposed to do. But it was all just bad luck. Sometimes it comes in bunches. It's all there as a matter of the public record. The coroner's office was informed. Community Services might even have looked into it."

"No autopsies, though," I says. "And it looks like the public record might not be complete."

"Who told you no autopsies?" Betancourt says, smiling a little sadly. "No autopsy on Mrs. Felton. No cause for suspicion when she died. Pill bottle wasn't found until after she was buried. Fact is, I don't think it was a bottle from which she got an overdose. I think it was just an old empty bottle she found somewhere and squirreled away as though it was a trinket. You know what I mean?"

I find myself nodding.

"But there was an autopsy on Mr. Felton. Hackman himself did the work and signed it off as accidental death."

"But nobody was made to answer for it?"

"We all answered for it, Jim. There was an accident. It shouldn't have happened. None of us working there at the time will ever stop wondering what simple thing we could've done to prevent the death. What-ifs don't do the job, though, do they, Jim? But maybe they help us do the job better from then on. So everybody keeps on trying. Me and Ms. Evergreen and Robert St. John and Mrs. Child and Jeannie Felton and Mr. Carmody."

"Carmody?" I says.

"Sure," he says, standing up and walking around his desk like he's sorry but he's got to end the interview. "Mr. Carmody's the ombudsman from the citizens' watchdog committee who's been looking us over for the last six months."

I stand up, and he takes my hand and holds onto it in a long shake while he's leading me to the door.

"That's right. Mr. Carmody's a relative of your good friend, Mr. Delvin, isn't he? Well, there you are. Knowing someone who cares is looking out for Mr. Delvin should put your heart to rest."

It don't put my heart to rest at all.

# 24

It's very hard nowadays to just walk into a doctor's office and expect to see the doctor, so I'm not surprised when I got to sit in Seltzer's waiting room for nearly the rest of the morning until he finally agrees to see me during what I figure is his coffee break.

He's a very neat-looking little man with rimless aviator-style eyeglasses, wearing a tan smock instead of a white one, which makes him look more like a barber than a doctor.

He's kicked back, sipping from a cup, when his receptionist shows me in and puts a card with my name on it on his desk. He don't get up or offer to shake hands but just leans forward to look at my name and to show me that he's alert. He asks me to have a seat.

"Oh, dear," he says, reaching for his intercom, "she forgot to bring in your medical record, Mr. Flannery."

"I didn't fill one out, doctor," I says. "I'm not here about my health."

There's a little change in his attitude, the way he's sitting. Like he tightens up. I can understand that with all the malpractice suits flying around, doctors must get very nervous when somebody comes to see them without being a patient. It could be a process server or a lawyer.

He don't even ask me what I'm there about but just raises his eyebrows a little bit.

148

"You know about Mr. Custer drowning over to the Larkspur Nursing Home?" I says.

"I didn't know. I'm no longer attending the people over there."

"Oh? How come is that?"

"Contract work for old-age facilities is not very remunerative. I took it on for two years because I wanted to make a contribution. But now the pressures of my own practice and the work I do two nights a week at the free clinic occupies all my time and more. Besides . . ."

"Besides what?"

"There's some satisfaction in working with the aged, but it's painful. It leaves you feeling very sad because you know that the most you can do is save a year or two for most of them. Make them a little more comfortable, perhaps."

"That seems a lot to me."

Seltzer gives me a quick smile like he appreciates the compliment but don't want to act giddy about it.

"Are you an ombudsman, Mr. Flannery?"

"No, sir. I'm a private citizen trying to find out a couple of things."

"What things?"

"The way they run Larkspur. The way they used to run it when the Feltons died."

He tightens up a little more. "Why?"

"Because I got a friend of mine in the home and I want to make sure what happened to them and Mr. Custer don't happen to him."

"Do you have any authority?"

"All I've got is my friendship for Mr. Delvin, and I figure that gives me all the authority I need."

"If you think there's danger, why don't you go to the police?"

"Because the police ain't really very interested."

"I don't know how I can help you, then. Everything I know is down on the record. I'm sure the police have a copy of the accident report that I filled out at the time of Mr. Felton's unhappy death."

"That's just it. I don't think a report was ever filed."

His lips get very thin. He moves them slightly like he's chewing on a sunflower seed.

"The Board of Health would know about that. They're the ones who'd make the determination if there was reason to inform the police."

"And I don't think an accidental death was filed on Mrs. Felton either."

"That wasn't an accidental death. It was death by heart failure."

"By an overdose of medicine."

"I couldn't swear to that. I didn't swear to it. That was never noted on the certificate of death. It could have been a misdosage, or it could have been the drug just had no effect any longer."

"Were you happy with the way Larkspur was run, Dr. Seltzer?"

"I don't imagine I'd be happy with the way most of the homes for the aged are run, Mr. Flannery. Everyone wants the best possible care. Nobody's willing to pay for it."

"So you won't say?"

"Are you suggesting that I was a conspirator in a plan to cheat the patients or defraud the state?"

"No, sir, I'm not. I just want to know what you thought about the home while you were the doctor."

He pauses for a long time, looking me over, wondering how far I'll run with whatever he decides to tell me, wondering if I'm a troublemaker who likes to rock boats or somebody who'll make waves where it'll do some good.

"If I had an aged relative, Mr. Flannery, I think I'd rather put them in a well-run kennel than into Larkspur the way it was run when the Feltons died."

# 25

With that thought in my head I go over to the Hall of Records. Jingles Finnegan is the man to see.

"I'd like to see the probate on one William Felton and one Lucy Felton."

"What business you got with them, Jimmy?"

"Just curiosity. Wills are a matter of public record, ain't they?"

"They go through probate, then anybody interested can take a look."

"So how come you're asking me what business I got with them?"

"Just curiosity," he says, and he grins at me.

He brings me back a copy of William Felton's will. "Lucy Felton's will ain't through probate yet," he says, "so you can't have a look at that."

"I expect we can pretty much tell what the entire estate's worth from what her husband left to her," I says.

William Felton don't leave Lucy Felton all that much. It looks to me that whatever they'd once owned had been eaten up by medical and nursing home expenses. Anyway, there's about a hundred thousand in cash and securities, plus a house and furniture. Say a quarter of a million altogether. There's a couple of bequests to charitable organizations, but nothing over five thousand dollars. Nothing's left to Larkspur. Nothing to Jeannie

Felton. Since Lucy outlives her husband by only a month, most of the quarter million's probably still intact.

"Lucy Felton's probate on the calendar?" I asks.

Finnegan looks up the calendar of the parts of the court.

"Probably coming out the middle of next week. Didn't the husband's will tell you what you want to know?"

"It told me that he left his wife some money. Now I got to find out who she left it to."

"Is it important?"

"It could be."

"Give me a minute."

He goes over in the corner and uses the phone. It takes him maybe five minutes.

When he comes back he says, "Lucy Felton left ten thousand to her niece, Jeannie Felton. The rest was left to the Antioch Missionary Baptist Church."

# 26

**M**r. Bikas, Mike, Mary, and me are sitting around the kitchen table again.

Mr. Bikas is telling me what I got to do as soon as the plans are approved and the building permit issued. He's also telling me what I can do even before that.

"You got to start lining up your subs," he says. "Your plumber, your electrician, your sheet metal, your drywall and plaster, your roofing, and your tile work. Then you got your mason, your sewer connection—"

Finally, I think, something I know a little something about.

"—your appliance broker, and your painter."

"Appliance broker?" I says.

"For your dishwasher, your cook top, your oven, and everything like that."

"I thought all you had to do was go down to the discount store and pick out what you want."

"That's one way. You watch the sales and compare prices a few places, that's one way. In fact, maybe it turns out to be the only way. You might not be able to find a broker willing to bid a small job like this. One house. How much commission can there be in one house for him? But you never know. You got to check it out. Save a dollar here, a dollar there."

"I got friends in every kind of business you can name, Mr. Bikas. I'm pretty sure I can go talk a deal."

"If you was going down to buy a new fridge from a friend, I'd say okay, you can maybe make yourself a good deal. But we're talking a new house here. You'd be surprised. Everybody sees a man's building a new house, they figure, what the hell, he's got money. A new house is like an apple tree. Everybody figures they got a right to give it a little shake. Don't ask me why. So you want to know about bids?"

I really don't, but I got to show some enthusiasm, so I hunch over my hands, which I got folded on the table in front of me, like some kid ready to learn his lessons.

"You want to get three—four's better—bids from every trade I named for you. So you line up three, four plumbing contractors, and you show them your funny papers."

"Plans," I says, informing Mary and Mike that I'm already into the jargon.

"Hey," Bikas says, and he grins like he's proud of his pupil. "With the plumber you tell him what kind of fixtures and finish."

He waits for me to explain, and when I don't explain he smiles like he's telling me I still got a lot to learn.

"Fixtures is like the kitchen sink, the bathroom basins, the toilets. Like that. Finish is the faucets and spigots. You understand? You got to look through the catalogs and make your choices. That could be fun for you."

It could be fun for him, maybe, but it wouldn't be fun for me. I hate to have to go shopping even for a pair of socks. But I glance at Mary, and I can see she thinks it's going to be fun.

"Now, you got to keep on these guys. They'll stall you."

"Why would they want to stall me? They bid for the job."

"They all bite off more than they can chew. You can't blame them. Say a contractor bids a job what won't start for sixty days, ninety days. He's got more work than he can handle, but sixty days, ninety days down the line, how does he know some job he's already got don't fall through? How does he know his lazy brother-in-law don't suddenly decide he wants to work, and the wife puts the pressure on him he should give her brother a job? So he bids the job, but until he signs the contract you don't know you really got him. And even then you can't be sure.

"Anyway he'll hold onto your funny papers one way or the other."

"How's that?"

"He knows funny papers cost you money. You're trying to save a dollar, so you ain't got a ton of them. You had maybe ten blueprinted. But the city wants two copies, water management wants a copy, the bank wants a copy, this and that. So the contractor figures, he holds onto your funny papers, maybe you run out and ain't got enough to get all the bids you want. It gives him a little edge. So maybe he does you the favor and comes here to the house to pick up a set of plans before he bids the job. After that you maybe got to chase after him to get them back."

Mary touches my hand. She can probably see all of this is giving me a headache. I ain't used to doing things this way, putting out bids and playing games.

Bikas is droning on how you compare the bids you get and you don't pick the low bid because it could mean the contractor intends to jerk you around and up the price after he's got the job, or it could mean he's going to cut a couple of corners. You don't take the high bid—the reason's obvious. So you take the best one of the other two as long as it's from a reputable man.

That I understand. That's the way I like to do business. Find an honest operator and sit down over a sandwich and say, "Look, this is what I want you to do. How much is it going to cost me?" And when he tells you, if you think it's too high or you know you can do better with somebody else, you say, "Is that the best you can do for me?" And you work it out.

So I says, "How come we don't do that right off the bat? Talk to somebody what comes recommended and cut a deal? I mean, you must know plenty of contractors you worked with before. Why can't we just sit down and talk to one of them?"

"Human nature," Bikas says, fixing me with this look like he's telling me how whatever else I'm going to learn from this house we're going to build together, here comes the most important lesson. "You got to keep people honest."

He looks me over and decides he's got to fill that out a little bit.

"Also you got to *help* people stay honest. You got to keep temptation away from them if you can. You understand what I'm saying?"

I nod my head. He thinks I'm saying I understand his lesson about contractors, but I'm really thinking about people like Evergreen and Carmody sitting there in the middle of this slush pile of welfare money, everybody crying poverty, and all kinds of people filling their pockets.

"Even honest people go bad around money," Bikas says.

# 27

D r. Henry Perkanola is the chief of medicine for the Health Department. But Mrs. Willamette Washington, administrator, runs the operation.

We got to be friends when I was looking into a situation that started when I was walking the sewers and found a man what was chewed in half by an alligator or some creature like that. She knows how to play the game, giving a little to get a little, but never sticking her head in the noose or her heart on her sleeve. It don't do no good to care so much you can't see your way around because you're blinded by tears, and she knows that.

"How can I help you, Jimmy?" she asks, after she offers me a seat and pours me a cup of orange spice tea. "Are you looking after someone in distress again?"

"A little information. All I want's a little information."

"You want to borrow from my bank?"

"I'll owe you, Willa. Whenever you want to call in the marker . . ." I wave my hand in the air, which means all she's got to do is make the call.

"What do you want to know?"

"How does the ombudsman program that watches over private hospitals and nursing homes work? How does somebody get appointed to it, for example?"

"The citizens' watchdog committee, which, as you know, has

157

no official or legal powers or duties and serves at the pleasure of the City Council, presents a list, compiled from recommendations of prominent citizens, every four years, or whenever a vacancy occurs, to the mayor's office."

"Is the list submitted at the start of each new administration?"

"No. Midterm. To avoid any wholesale partisan replacement. The impression meant to be given, more or less accurately, is that the ombudsmen are above the political fray."

"Are they?"

"By and large. But Jimmy, you know and I know, whenever anybody serves in public office, elective, appointive, or hired, somebody's going to work some politics. Whenever one group of people have the least bit of power over any other people, there's going to be wheeling and dealing."

"So the mayor makes the appointments?"

"The mayor's office, which isn't the same thing. It's usually too ordinary a matter for the mayor to bother with, unless somebody wants a favor or something goes sour. He hands it to his executive assistant, who hands it to an aide, who hands one copy to the Commission on Human Relations, another copy to the Department of Health, and another copy to the Association of Health and Hospital Services."

"The people that're going to be watched get to have a say about who watches them?"

"Nothing wrong with that, Jimmy. Every list has no fewer than seven names for each vacancy. It's always possible that somebody on the full list might have it in for a hospital or a nursing home. Something personal. The facilities have a right to strike off two names for each vacancy."

"Like choosing a jury?"

"Something like. Then we vet the list and strike off anyone we know or suspect to be incompetent."

"Who investigates?"

"Our own staff."

"Which is overworked."

"Very."

"So you get out the old rubber stamp."

"Since we're not in on the final selection, that's the way it usually works. That's the way nearly everything in government works, so don't look so disapproving."

"What does the job pay?"

"A token. A hundred dollars a month. I'm sure it doesn't even cover the cost of gasoline."

"So I wonder why anybody would want to go through the trouble to get a job like that."

"To do a little bit of good, maybe?"

"The character I'm wondering about, one Francis Carmody, don't impress me that he's got charity in his heart."

"One never knows. I know a tough, redheaded little Irishman who looks like he'd rather punch you in the mouth than give you a hand, who's always spending his time and his money helping people."

I know I'm turning red, and she's getting a kick out of it.

"What kind of schedule do they have to keep?"

"There is no schedule. The ombudsmen inspect when they choose to inspect."

"They have to announce themselves?"

"They don't have to, but sooner or later they have to show their credentials. Otherwise they'd never be allowed to go into places visitors weren't allowed."

"But that would be giving warning."

"If a place is a mess, it can't be cleared up in five minutes while the ombudsman's being stalled at the door."

"They could be shown what the staff wanted them to see. Potemkin's village."

She raises her eyebrows like she's surprised I should know about such things.

"They're pretty well trained and soon learn all the tricks they don't teach in school. They're hard to fool."

"So they go now and then, this place and that place. No pattern?"

"That's right. The only requirement is that they visit each facility at least once a month."

"Does anybody check to see they done it?"

She spins her Rolodex and writes down a name, number, and address on a piece of notepaper.

"You can contact Mrs. Harriet Blalock. She's the current president of the ombudsmen. She keeps the records as they're turned in each month. She can give you details I don't have."

"Do you think she can tell me who recommended the appointees?"

"I might be able to do that for you," Willamette says. She gets up and goes to a filing cabinet. "As long as the appointment was made within the last three years."

She goes through the files looking for Carmody's name.

"Here it is," she says. "He was appointed to fill a vacancy only last year. Fourteen months ago."

"Who sponsored him?"

"Wally Dunleavy, Jack Reddy—"

"The superintendent of the water department?"

"That's right," she says. "And . . ." She hesitates.

"And?" I says.

"Henry Perkanola."

It's quiet for a minute, and then I asks, "Do you think I could have a word with Dr. Perkanola?"

"He's not in, Jimmy."

"You're not pulling up the drawbridge, are you?"

"I think he should know you've shown an interest in his endorsement of this Carmody before you walk in on him."

"That's all it is right now, an interest. Just an interest. You think your colleague needs time to make up a story, maybe it becomes a suspicion."

"You're putting pressure on me, Jimmy."

"That ain't what I want to do. I just don't see the difficulty. I talked to Dr. Perkanola plenty of times before."

"He's having a late lunch."

"You happen to know where he catches a bite?"

"At a place called the Irish Pub just down the street."

# 28

I know the Irish Pub pretty good. It's owned and operated for the last ten, twelve years by a Jew by the name of Moe Shoenberg. Everybody calls Moe "Snowbird" because he turns the restaurant over to his son-in-law and goes to Florida the first time the snow flies.

It's not a very big place. It's crowded like it's always crowded from the minute it opens at six in the morning to the minute it closes twelve at night. I order a pastrami on rye with coleslaw and a pickled tomato side, also a Dr. Brown's cream soda, from Snowbird's daughter, who's got a face as round as a knish and a smile that makes people laugh.

When it's ready, I stand there with the tray in my hands, looking over the tables.

I spot Dr. Perkanola hunched over his plate, shoveling it in. I notice that doctors ain't always got the best table manners, maybe because they're so busy they got to eat fast when they get the chance.

He looks up when I ask him if I can share his table.

"Go ahead and sit, Flannery. Is this a coincidence?"

"No."

"I didn't think so. You're causing trouble over at Larkspur Nursing."

"Who told you that?"

"The word gets around."

"Well, you're right about that."

"Don't pussyfoot, Flannery. Come out with it."

"I was wondering how come, with all the complaints I hear about that place, you ain't closed them down."

"If we closed down every hospital, day care center, rest home, convalescence home, and nursing home that has complaints filed against it, people would be dying in the streets. Don't you get it?"

"Get what?"

"Get how things really are. How things really work. You political types give me a laugh. You think the board of supervisors, the state legislature, the United States Congress passes some laws, and that's all there is to that. Problem solved. Well, that's not all there is to that. Next you got to write the statutes and ordinances. Then you got to pass appropriations. Then you got to get an executive order to get the money out of the treasury. Federal, state, or city, it doesn't matter. Now you got the money, so you think everything's hunky-dory, right? Not right. You can't just throw money at problems like poverty, and old age, and catastrophic illness. You've got to build the right facilities. You've got to maintain them. You've got to staff them. You've got to monitor them to see nobody's got their hand in the till up to the elbow."

I'm sitting there in amazement, not interrupting, not even trying to slow down the tide, while Perkanola delivers me this lecture at high speed while he's eating his corned beef and noodles without missing a chew or hardly taking a breath.

"You set up committees to watch committees to watch committees to watch everything and everybody. You end up with more layers of administration than an Eskimo's got on sweaters in the middle of winter. You end up spending five times as much for the people watching the people supposed to do the job as for the people who are actually doing the job.

"And it doesn't do a hell of a lot of good, because standards are set impossibly high, and the people we can afford to hire have performance that's impossibly low. Then there's human nature, which teaches us that in every ten people we got eight honest, one crooked, and one marginal. Then we got inefficiency and weariness and burnout and professional shell shock and what the hell all.

"On top of which, people who can't even balance their own checkbook or change a light bulb get all bent out of shape because a thousand here, a thousand there, out of hundreds of thousands, slip through the cracks and an overworked, half-trained care giver messes up on a dose of medication, pushes the wrong button on a dialysis machine, or leaves somebody in the bath for a minute without supervision."

He finally runs down.

"I don't know about any dialysis machine," I says, "but you got two out of three."

"What?"

"The man who died in the bathtub and the woman who got the wrong amount of the right medicine."

"I don't know what you're talking about."

"Sure you do. You know what I'm talking about or two out of three wouldn't've popped up in that speech you just gave me. You know I'm talking about the Feltons."

He stops eating and just stares at me with this sadness in his face. "That their names? That the names of that man and wife who died at Larkspur?"

"Are you kidding me, doctor? You telling me you don't know their names?"

"Guess how many names I see on death certificates sent to my office from hospitals and nursing homes. Guess how many."

"I wouldn't know how to start counting."

"That's right. But I know how many. And guess how many of those deaths could probably be deemed preventable."

I just sit there.

"Don't know how to start counting them, either? Of course you don't. Just people like me and Mrs. Willamette know, and we can't do a damn thing about it. Listen to what I'm telling you, Flannery. There's too damn many people, and nobody takes care of his own anymore."

"Everything you say is true. I know that. But I'm just looking at the Larkspur and what happened there."

"Because Delvin's there."

"That's right. Because I'm trying to take care of my own, just like you say most people ain't doing. And there's one other thing."

"Yes?" He's staring at me, focusing on a spot right between my eyes like he'd like to shoot me right there for what he knows I'm about to say.

"You got an interest in Fair Winds Incorporated, what owns and runs the Larkspur Nursing Home, and from where I stand, politician or no politician, it looks like conflict of interest to me."

"Is that all?" he asks, like he's telling me to go away. "For Christ's sake, Flannery, the Catholic Church and the Chicago Federation of Hebrew Congregations are invested in nursing homes, too. It's business. It hasn't got anything to do with anything except business."

I can't argue that. Anybody who buys a share, invests a dollar in a big company, could be investing in poison gas, strip mining, acid rain. Who knows? I suppose he's right. You can't go around checking up on what every dollar you got invested for your old age is doing even if it's crapping up somebody else's old age.

# 29

$M$rs. Blalock keeps an office in her high-rise condominium on the Gold Coast by the lake.

She's got a secretary, a maid, two corgis—the favorite dog of Queen Elizabeth, according to what I read—and at least a cook. When I'm shown into the room where she's sitting behind a desk—what probably costs about as much as the house I'm planning to build is going to cost—she asks me if I'd like some tea. When I says I could use a cup of coffee, she tells her secretary, Emily, to ask Molly to brew a pot of each and make a tray of sandwiches.

When I tell her I already had my lunch she smiles and says, "If you don't want to eat, you don't have to eat. You can watch me."

There's some people got money do things like that and make you feel small. Other people got money do things like that and make you feel good. Mrs. Blalock's the second type.

She's about sixty—looking fifty—with her gray hair done in some soft way that frames her face without making it look like she's trying to be girlish. She's wearing a yellow dress, there's yellow roses in vases on tables here and there, the heavy velvet drapes are yellow, and there's a painting of daffodils on the wall in the best spot, where it'll catch the light but not the sun. It's like sitting in a field of buttercups.

"It's very good of you to see me on such short notice," I says.

"Your reputation goes before you, Mr. Flannery."

"Reputation?"

"For helping out your fellow man when and where you can."

"Well . . ." I says, tongue-tied for no reason I can figure out.

"I've made you uncomfortable," she says. "I'm sorry."

"It ain't that, Mrs. Blalock. I suppose I like a pat on the back the same as anybody else, but when somebody says it out loud it makes you wonder if you do what you can because you want to do what you can or because somebody'll say what a nice guy you are."

"I understand exactly what you mean. I have people—some are even friends—who call me a busybody and a do-gooder behind my back." She laughs like she thinks that's funny. "Some don't even wait until my back is turned."

The maid comes in with a wheeled cart. There's a silver tray on it with two pots, one for coffee and one for tea, and a plate of sandwiches. They ain't them little bites with the crust cut off, you got to pop three or four in your mouth before you got enough to chew, they're regular sandwiches, corned beef and cheese on rye. Pickles on the side.

I can't resist. I take a sandwich and watch her pour.

"For heaven's sake, loosen your tie and kick back," she says. "Now tell me what I can do for you."

"It's about the ombudsmen."

"Yes, what about them?"

"You know every one of them pretty good?"

"Before or after their appointment?"

"Either. Both." I take a bite of sandwich. It's even got a thin layer of coleslaw on it. It's even better than the one I had at the Irish Pub.

She takes a sip of tea and says, "The hell with this," punches a button, and tells the secretary through the intercom that we'd like a couple of beers. I hold up my hand.

"Wait a minute, Emily," she says. "No beer, Mr. Flannery?"

"I got no head for alcoholic beverages."

"What's your pleasure? A sandwich like this deserves more than a cup of coffee or tea."

"You wouldn't happen to have a Dr. Brown's?"

"Cream or Cel-Ray?"

"Cream."

"Make that one beer and one Dr. Brown's cream, Emily," she says. She lets go the switch and says, "You spend much time in New York, Mr. Flannery?"

"It's Jimmy, if that's okay with you. No. Chicago's the biggest town I want to hang around."

"Should have been the principal city of the nation. Principal city of the world," she says, nodding her head like she's agreeing with me that Chicago's all the city anybody should want. "But government kept their eyes on Europe the first couple of hundred years, and they'll be keeping them on Asia the next couple of hundred, when all the time they should have been looking out from the heartland, north and south, Canada and Mexico and beyond. But New York invented Dr. Brown's, so that's worth something. By the way, it's Harriet. Now, where were we?"

"How well do you know the other ombudsmen?"

"Most of them are old friends of mine. All of those that have put in any kind of service at all."

"Is Francis Carmody an old friend?"

"I scarcely knew him when his name was put up for consideration. One of the people who sponsored him, Jack Reddy, was an old, old friend, however."

"The superintendent of the Water Department?" I says.

"That's right. Do you know him?"

"We've said hello and split a rubber chicken at some fund-raiser a time or two," I says.

"My husband went to high school with Jack." She smiles. "I was born to this, but my late husband wasn't. He was a self-made man. Just like Jack Reddy."

A little frown pops up on her smooth forehead.

"What is it?" I says.

She waves her hand as though brushing a fly away. "Oh, nothing. For some reason I was just about to say, 'Like Francis Carmody,' but I don't know why."

"Well, you made a connection. You were talking about your husband and Jack Reddy both being self-made men, and that made you think of Carmody. Is he a self-made man?"

"That's just it. He pretends to be. Perhaps he is, but in what way? He's a common huckster, isn't he? Sells wholesale novelties? Pens with women printed on them that lose their bathing suits when you turn the pens upside down. Dribble glasses. Little plastic messes you can put on the carpet if you've got that kind of sense of humor. Don't misunderstand me, Jimmy, there's nothing wrong with being a huckster. And nothing wrong in being common. It's the two things together that give me an uneasy feeling about Mr. Carmody. I hear rumors."

"What sort of rumors, Harriet?"

"Rumors that he's been doing very well indeed the last few months. One wonders how being a volunteer ombudsman would improve a common huckster's fortunes."

She puts down the part of the sandwich she ain't finished and wipes her fingers on a napkin.

"That may have sounded condescending, Jimmy. Patronizing. I didn't mean it to be. It's my opinion. It's what I feel.

"When you're born to wealth and privilege it's as though you give up your right to be disapproving of people less fortunate than you. You're not even supposed to say what you think about the climbers and the wheeler-dealers. You're not supposed to doubt their honesty and sincerity.

"Mr. Carmody makes me suspect his motives. Princes have been born in shanties, but Mr. Carmody's tales of poverty seem like fictions to me."

"Lies?"

"That's right. Self-serving lies. He rattles off his relationship with your Mr. Delvin a little too glibly. Do you know what I mean? He recites his family tree as though he's memorized it."

I chew that one over along with a bite of sandwich.

"Does he do what he's supposed to do for your organization?"

She reaches for the intercom switch and asks Emily for the file on Mr. Carmody.

"How many institutions is each ombudsman required to watch over?" I asks while we're waiting.

"A dozen, more or less. That's enough. A visit once a month can steal most of your evenings and weekends."

Emily comes in with the file and puts it on the expensive table.

Mrs. Blalock leafs through it after putting on a pair of rimless glasses.

"Well, not as bad as I thought. In the five months since he's been with us, he seems to have done his share."

"How long has he been assigned to Larkspur?"

"Since he started with us. Almost six months."

"Did his reports on conditions there start out bad and then start getting good?"

"They did, so perhaps his scrutiny is doing some good."

When I don't agree to that she asks, "What's the matter?"

"Well, I don't know what it was like six months ago, but two people died under doubtful circumstances since then, and another one died just the other day."

"I've heard."

"And from what I can see, the life for most of the old people over to the Larkspur ain't no bed of roses."

I can't think of anything else, so I stand up and thank her for the sandwich, the Dr. Brown's, and her time.

She sees me to the door herself.

"Did you ever think of being an ombudsman, Jimmy?" she asks.

"I'm a Democratic Party precinct captain, Harriet, and maybe that's pretty much what I'm doing."

# 30

When I get home, Stanley Recore, the little kid what lives across the hall, is sitting on the stoop. Except he's not a little kid anymore. He must be ten or eleven. I mean he ain't exactly grown up, but he's stretching out, he ain't a puppy no more.

He's losing this funny way of talking he used to have, but whenever he's upset and trying to hide it, it comes back.

"Jimbly," he says, hugging his knees and looking up at me from underneath his eyebrows. "Is wha' I hear de troot?"

"Whattaya hear, Stanley?"

"That you an' Mawy and Alfie is goin' to move away."

"Who told you that?"

"Mrs. Blini tol' me dat. Pearl an' Joe tol' me dat. Myron an' Shirley tol' me dat."

"You going to name everybody in the building?" I asks.

He acts like he don't even hear me but goes right on. "Miz Foowan and Miz King tol' me dat. Miz Warnowski tol' me dat."

"Mrs. Warnowski don't even live in the building anymore, Stanley. Mrs. Bilina lives in her old apartment."

"I know dat. Mrs. Warnowski come to visit. My mother and father tol' me you was movin' away, too. Also my sister."

"So everybody in the building's heard about it," I says.

"Is it twoo?"

170

"Mary and me are thinking of building a house over by Horan Park."

"My God, that's fi' blocks away," he says.

"That's right. It's only five blocks from here. You want to see Alfie or Mary, all you got to do is take a little stroll."

"A wittle stwoll?" he says, offended by my attitude. "Tha's pracally halfway 'cross da town."

"You walk farther than that when you take Alfie for a walk," I says, sitting down next to him.

"We never walk over by that old park," he says, making a case that's sensible to him.

"Well, if you won't walk over and see us, Stanley, we'll walk over and see you."

He jumps off the stoop and stands there like he's ready to face the world alone if he's got to.

"Hellofa time to go runnin' out on your frens, tha's all I got to say," he says.

"What're you talking about?"

"Ever'body got notice. I bet you look in the mailbox you'll see you got notice, too."

He walks away on me in a hurry before I can ask him any more questions.

So I go into the grocery store.

Joe Pakula's standing behind the counter all by hisself.

"What's Stanley talking about everybody got their notice?" I asks.

"Ain't you got yours yet?" he says. "Somebody's buying up the block. Going to turn all the six flats into condos. We all been given notice we got sixty days to move."

# 31

Mary's going on nights, so Mike and me decide to go over to the Sold Out Saloon, like we used to do practically every Wednesday night before I got married, and have ourselves a sausage and cabbage feed.

Also I want to talk to him about what I found out about the building being sold.

It looks like old Mr. Stumpnagler, what's owned the building ever since I can remember, has had a couple of years of bad luck, his wife dying being the topper.

"You heard about the building being sold?" I asks my father.

"Sure, I heard."

"Sixty days notice, they give everybody."

"That don't mean nothing. That's just how lawyers do it. The way I figure we got seven, eight months. You'll have your house built. Stumpnagler ain't even accepted an offer yet."

"I know that. I went over to talk to him the minute I heard about the notices."

"So? Then he told you. What'd he tell you?"

I tell Mike what Mr. Stumpnagler told me.

"I'm past seventy, Jimmy," Stumpnagler says. "What am I gonna do, sweat to death in summer and freeze to death in winter for the rest of my life? It's time I had a little pleasure for myself.

Sell what I got. Take a little cruise. Buy myself a condo in Florida."

"It gets very hot in Florida, too, Mr. Stumpnagler, and they also got cockroaches as big as mice."

"All right," he says. "I'll go to New Orleans."

"Also hot and humid, with mice as big as cats."

"You're trying to discourage me," Mr. Stumpnagler says. "So California. I'll run up and down the seashore until I find a town ain't got any cockroaches, ain't got any mice." He reaches out and touches my hand. "I'm tired, Jimmy. Maybe all I do is sell up and buy myself into the best retirement home with pretty nurses and twenty-four-hour doctors in attendance. You know, Jimmy, I never thought I'd want to live forever, but now, even with all the pain, with all the loneliness, I think I would. So maybe money can buy me a little bit of forever, what do you think?"

"I think you got a right. But I'm wondering if we can't find a way to save the building for the people what live in it."

"You talk about the building like I owned fifty like it. That's my fortune, Jimmy. That and the bungalow me and Molly lived in for thirty years. That's it. That's my nest egg. What do you want me to do, give it away?"

"I didn't say that."

"What do you care? You'll be starting to build your own house over by the park pretty soon. So you won't even be around to see the old building change."

"I'm thinking about my neighbors."

"I know you are. They don't make them like you anymore, Jimmy. You care about people."

"Don't say things like that, Mr. Stumpnagler. You're embarrassing me."

"So, you're embarrassed to be a good boy? You're embarrassed to care about your friends. Huh? Huh?"

"I'm starting to feel foolish," I tell my old man. "Mr. Stumpnagler's going on like this. Then finally he says, 'I tell you what. You find me a down payment for the building. A hundred thousand. Enough for me to do this or that. I'll carry your paper. You don't even got to scramble for a bank loan, which you couldn't qualify for anyway.' "

"Did you tell him he might as well ask you for fifty million?" Mike says. "Where you going to get that kind of money?"

I don't answer him right away.

"What are you sitting there saying nothing for?" he asks.

"I talked to Itzy Dumkowski on the phone. He guarantees the lot Mrs. Banjo left me could bring thirty thousand. Maybe thirty-two five."

"So?" Mike says, sitting there looking at me dumbfounded, his face getting red.

"I also talked to Joe and Pearl Pakula. They got maybe ten, twenty thousand saved up. And the Shapiros, Myron and Shirley—"

"I know who is the Shapiros," Mike says.

"—got a little put away."

"You're talking about forgetting about the house? You're talking about selling the lot Mrs. Banjo gives you?" he says, his voice starting to go up like it does when he's ready to give me an argument.

"Where's Miss King and Mrs. Foran going to go?" I says, my voice going up, too. "You want them to be welfare patients in a nursing home? How about Mrs. Bilina? How about the Recores, for that matter?"

"Ah, it was your mother—God rest her soul—raised you to kindness and generosity, Jim, but now—"

"And so did you. So did you."

"—I wonder if we really did right by you. Have you talked to Mary?"

"I'm going to talk to her the first chance I get."

"I think I'll have a beer," my father says, "you've got me so upset."

"I'll join you," Joe Medill, who happens to be passing by just that minute, says.

Jackie Boyle's right behind him, grinning over his shoulder.

It's their week to be pals.

"Let's sit right down here and join the Flannerys," Medill says. "Let's discuss ways and means. Lets talk of who, what, why, where, when, and how."

"What're you rattling on about?" Mike says.

"The makings of a news story."

"The contents of a news story's first paragraph. Remember this. When all else confuses, ask yourself these simple questions."

"Who, what, why, where, when, and how!" the two of them sing out like they was a vaudeville act.

# 32

Mary comes home by twelve-thirty, and we're in bed by one.

The pastrami, coleslaw, and pickled tomato from the Irish Pub is talking to the corned beef, cheese, and pickles from Mrs. Blalock's, which is having a conversation with the kielbasa and cabbage from Dan Blatna's Sold Out Saloon.

Even though I'm wide awake at three o'clock, Mary don't stir. Changing the shift always knocks the starch out of her, and she sleeps like a log the first eight hours she comes back from work. Even so, I move my leg every once and a while so she won't think she's sleeping next to a corpse and wake up.

I'm thinking about who, what, where, why, and how.

I'm thinking I ain't got many facts pinned down, just a lot of people running around acting this way and that way, ways you wouldn't expect them to act.

There's Evergreen, who acts like a school principal one minute and a vamp the next—but maybe I just *think* she acts like a vamp because Mrs. Child puts the thought in my head—who runs around in tailored suits with black stockings and garter belts underneath her bathrobe. Who goes right back to the pond when I appear at the door saying there's a dead body on the grounds. Who's maybe having a little roll in the hay with the big Trinidadian who, what with the scar on his face, might look like a killer—which I understand is very attractive to some women—but might

176

be a pussycat—the seduc*ee* instead of the seduc*er*. Then there's little Jeannie Felton, who—it looks to me—was a pretty faithful and affectionate niece to the Feltons, but who got left with only a taste of the pie.

And there was Mrs. Child, who's pretty good at soaking hankies, but who's a tattletale and very good at playing on a person's heartstrings. Who could also be the kind that watches and waits for the opportunity to do a person she don't like an injury.

And there's Jack Boxer, who's supposed to be such a good care giver but who goes around shouting in the faces of old men and raising his hand to them like he's going to hit them.

There's pretty dark-skinned women tying an old woman with a mouth like a docker down to the bed, and another woman talking about mice, and an old man borrowing a lady's bathrobe so he can go steal streusel buns and get hisself drowned in three inches of water around the edge of a duck pond, and the ducks what was having lunch on his hair, and rats. And a forty-inch color television set. And a member of the board who likes to play good ol' boy. And politicians who put their retirement money into nursing homes. And doctors who do the same. And this character Francis Carmody, who could be the biggest thief and con merchant of the bunch with his plastic pens filled with naked women, who got hisself named Delvin's guardian when he maybe ain't even a relative.

And there's my old Chinaman, Chips Delvin, lying there breathing through his mouth, fed like a baby, so ga-ga he thinks I'm his pop, getting so thin and weak I'm afraid he's going to go to his reward in heaven—or whatever—any minute.

Which decides me. The hell with trying to figure it all out. When you don't know what to do, you got to listen to your heart.

I get out of bed and start throwing on my clothes.

That wakes Mary up, and she says, "What are you doing now, James?"

And I says, "I'm going over to get Delvin out of that snake pit and bring him home."

She don't argue. She just says, "Be careful and hurry back. I'll make up the couch."

# 33

I take Alfie along in case I need a cover story again.

"What we're doing is probably very dumb," I says, "but I can't let my old Chinaman stay in that place another hour."

He gives me a little whine like he's agreeing with me.

I park the car at the curb on the street in back under the canopy of trees. The neighborhood's so quiet you can practically hear the people breathing inside their bedrooms and stirring in their sleep.

"I don't got to tell you not to upset the ducks, do I?" I says, and Alfie gives me a look like he's ashamed of me asking such a question from an old nighthawk like him.

I get a flashlight and an old trench coat out of the trunk.

There's not much of a moon, though the night's clear, and I can even see some stars directly overhead where the city shine don't wash them out. Alfie and me come out of the shelter of trees to the edge of the lawn. The ducks is quiet. The house is dark except for the dim light I know comes from the front where the desk is. We trot across the lawn, hunkered down like a couple of thieves.

I tell Alfie to wait for me at the door to the cellar. He sits down and looks around like he's giving the area the eye.

I get into Larkspur through the basement, the same way I done before. I snap on the flashlight and make my way across the cement floor to the staircase. I tiptoe up the steps, the big old house snapping and popping all around me, and jimmy the door at the top.

That's the first time and place where a little bit of bad luck could do me in. It's a long shot, but somebody could be walking by just that second while I'm fiddling with the lock or while I'm opening the door a crack to see if the way is clear. Nobody's there. I'm inside the house without a bit of trouble.

I walk down the hall until I can look around the bend and see who I got to contend with in case Delvin makes a row and brings the night attendant running. Mrs. Child is sitting at the desk reading a book.

Somebody moans from somewhere in the house, and she lifts her head, listening to see if there's going to be more. But the moan don't come again, and she looks at her watch and then goes back to the book.

I go back to Delvin's room, open the door, and slip inside. It's as dark as the inside of a black cat's belly.

Shielding the flash with my fingers so only a little light peeks through, I locate myself and go over to the bed.

Delvin's lying on his back, his mouth open wide again. I move the flash and find the glass with his teeth in it. I go fish them out so I'll have them ready when I wake him up. Then I look for his clothes in the closet, but there ain't any in there, which is what I figured and why I brought along the coat. But I find a pair of his slippers on the floor.

Finally I go back to the bed and sit on it so I can bend over and look into his face while I poke him as easy as I can and still wake him. It takes maybe a minute before he opens his eyes.

"What the hell's going on?" he says, like he's got a mouthful of mush.

"Here's your teeth, Mr. Delvin," I says.

He fumbles around in the air in front of his face. Between us we get his teeth in his mouth like you'd bit a horse.

"Pop, is that you?" he asks.

I shine the light in my own face from under my chin.

"You look a sight, Pop. Have you been ill?" he says.

"I'm feeling better. Are you strong enough to take a little walk with me?"

"What time of day is it?"

"It's early morning."

"How early?"

"About three-thirty A.M."

"Why in God's name would I be wanting to take a little walk at three-thirty in the A.M.?"

"There's something I'd like you to take a look at. Here. Let's see if we can sit you up."

He lets me do that. I throw the covers back off his legs and stand up so I can move his legs over to the side of the bed.

"I've been having dreams, Pop," he says.

"Bad dreams?" I asks, putting the slippers on his feet.

"Good and bad."

"Well, we all have our share," I says, managing to help him slide off the edge of the bed so his feet are on the floor. In another second he's standing up. He's tottering a little and leaning on my shoulder, but at least he's on his feet.

"Not like some of the dreams I've been having," he says. "Terrible things. You know what, Pop?"

"What?" I says, getting his arms through the armholes of the coat.

"I think I been dead and come back to life. Am I going mad?"

"No, you ain't going mad," I says while we try a couple of steps toward the door. "You was like dead, but you're coming back to life right now, I can tell you that."

"Jesus, Mary, and Joseph, my legs is weak."

"Understandable," I says, opening the door, "but I think if we said a prayer, you'd be strong enough to make it out the door."

We're out the door and across the hall, almost to the basement door, before he says, "What prayer did you have in mind?"

"The Lord is my shepherd is always a good one."

" 'The Lord is my shepherd—' "

"Could we have a silent prayer?" I whispers.

He clams up, and we're through the door and at the top of the cellar steps.

"Can't do it, Pop. It's too far down there," he says.

"Just say the prayer," I says.

He sits down on the step halfway down, and I can't stop him.

I'm strong enough—what with him losing so much weight—but he's a lot taller than me, and if he wants to sit, there's not much I can do about it.

"I don't want to take a walk," he says. "I just want to go back to my bed."

"You got to at least give it a try."

"What for?"

"For me."

"I can hardly see who you are, it's so dark."

"Wait a second," I says. I take the chance. I run up to the top of the stairs and turn on the light, then I hurry back and squat beside him.

"Jimmy! What the hell are you doing wandering around my bedroom? Did Mrs. Banjo let you in?"

"She's waiting down in the parlor."

I help him to his feet. We make it to the bottom of the stairs.

"What's she waiting for?" he asks.

"She wants to have a chat."

Before you know it we're across the cellar and at the outside door. I snap off the light at the switch. We go out into the back yard.

Alfie gets up and walks along beside us as we make our way across the lawn toward the pond and the trees. This is the second place we could be spotted, because we're out in the open for so long.

But we make that, too.

"Where are we, Jimmy?" Delvin asks.

"We just left the Larkspur Nursing Home," I says.

"I mean what's with all the trees? We on a fishing trip in the woods?"

"No. We're right in the middle of Chicago."

"I'll be damned."

Then we're out of the trees and into the car. He practically collapses against the door. He's in Alfie's seat, so Alfie gets up on his lap.

"Mrs. Banjo's dead," he says.

"Yes."

"So where are we really going, Jimmy?"

"I'm taking you home," I says.
I run around and get behind the wheel.
"This beast just licked my face," Delvin says.
"I'm sorry."
"Oh, that's all right," he says.
I start the car, and we drive off.

# 34

Delvin's all tucked in under the comforter, fast asleep on the couch in the living room.

I don't know if the exercise and the night air shocked him sensible a little, but he recognizes Mary right off, so it seems to me he's already improved.

Mary and me are sitting out at the kitchen table having a cup of tea.

"He's been given drugs," Mary says.

"They been feeding them to him ever since he arrived at that place."

"We'll have Dr. Chapman look him over in the morning."

I nod my head.

"You look all worn out, James."

"Well, it's not the running around tonight that's got me frayed," I says.

Mary waits for me to tell her what's got me frayed, but I'm afraid to bring it up.

Finally she says, "The house, James?"

"What?"

"Have you been worried about telling me we're not going to build the house?"

"You know what's going on with the building?"

"Mike's told me all about Mr. Stumpnagler wanting to sell out and go to some place in the sunbelt. About the offer he made you."

"Mary, I want what you want."

She reaches out and takes my hand. "And I want what you want."

"So where does that leave us?"

"I think, if the finances can be arranged, it leaves us right here on Polk Street for a while."

"It won't be forever."

"I don't know if it matters all that much. Favor for favor?"

"What's that?"

"You keep on loving me, and I'll be happy living just about anywhere," she says.

I look into my teacup because I don't want Mary to see I got tears in my eyes.

# 35

I wait for Dr. Chapman to come over and have a look at Delvin.

When he's finished he comes out in the kitchen and says, "He's been given drugs, that's for certain. Tranquilizers and sedatives for certain. The effects of those are starting to wear off. Psychedelics, too, I'm willing to bet."

"He's okay otherwise?"

"Weak as a kitten, but I suppose you already know that if you got him from the nursing home to here last night."

"So all he needs is some rest?"

"Forget the rest. He needs exercise. Naturally, you shouldn't overdo it until he starts getting stronger. It's amazing how quickly the muscles will waste away when they're not being used. Get him up, out, and walking around this morning. Again this afternoon, and tonight as well."

"How about diet?" Mary asks.

"What he can take. Plenty of strong broth to start. Solid food as soon as his stomach will tolerate it. He hasn't been starved, but the next thing to it. This all happened to him at the nursing home?"

"That's where it happened."

"It's getting really bad, isn't it?" Dr. Chapman says. "The care givers aren't giving care anymore."

After he leaves I go into the living room to see how Delvin's doing.

"There you are, Jimmy," he says.

"How are you feeling?"

"Better. Have I been sick?"

"You were sad about Mrs. Banjo, and somebody took advantage."

"That cousin of mine?"

"He signed you into that nursing home and kept you there when I wanted to get you out."

"So how did you manage my escape?"

"In the dead of night."

"How did you manage to get in?"

"Picked some locks."

"Thank God you're such a rascal, Jimmy."

I'm ready to go when he reaches out and takes my sleeve to keep me there a moment more.

"Jimmy."

"Yes, sir."

"I thought I heard you and Mary talking around the kitchen table."

"Yes?"

"Were you talking about raising the money to buy this building?"

"We were."

"I thought so. I wasn't sure was I hearing right or was I dreaming. So, Jimmy, what I want to say is I'm ready to make up the difference of what you can get from the other tenants and what you need to make the deal."

I feel like crying again. Delvin's famous for being so tight with a nickel that he squeezes it until the Indian's riding the buffalo, and here he is offering to lend us a considerable piece of change.

Then he says, "About the interest. Regular bank rates'll do."

I drive over to the Larkspur with Alfie. There's a couple of who, what, why, where, when, and hows I want to clear up. Like what did Mr. Custer tell Mrs. Spencer when he came to borrow her robe? Like why was St. John walking around the pond when he was standing guard? Like how did Evergreen know that the body was back by the pond when I came to the door to say I'd found one, and why was she so shocked to find out it was Mr. Custer in Mrs. Spencer's robe? Like who slammed the car door half a block down the street at three-thirty in the morning? Like where was Jack Boxer when Mr. Felton drowned and Mr. Felton took too much heart medicine and Mr. Custer fell into the duck pond? Like when did all these accidents start happening?

I know the answer to the last one. They started happening when Evergreen arrived on the job.

When I walk up the path to the front door, I notice that Agnes Spencer is one of the old people dressing up the glassed-in sun porch.

St. John's on the desk. He starts getting up when he sees me walk in, but I hold up my hand like I'll get to him in a minute and go out on the porch to talk to Mrs. Spencer.

She's sitting in an easy chair, watching some talk show on the television.

I walk over and sit down beside her.

"Anything good on the television?"

"It's awful."

"So why are you sitting here watching it?"

"Well, it's better than sitting in my room all alone."

I got nothing to say to that.

"You ought to get out a little, maybe."

She looks at me very quick and says, "You offering?"

"Sure. One of these days I'll come over and we'll take a walk down to Micek Park and sit under the trees."

She looks at me very smug. "Don't bother. I got somebody taking me on an outing tomorrow morning."

"One of your relatives?"

"I got none to speak of."

"One of your old friends, then."

"Jeannie. Jeannie Felton. She's taking me out in a paddle boat in the lagoon in Jackson Park tomorrow at ten."

"Hey, that's nice, maybe take a little swim?"

She shakes her head. "Oh, I can't swim."

"So maybe you shouldn't be taking a row on the lake."

"Jeannie says she's a very good swimmer and I'm not to worry."

"About the other night when Mr. Custer came to borrow your bathrobe?"

She looks away from me in a hurry, like the television's suddenly doing something very interesting.

"Mrs. Spencer?"

She don't look at me.

"Why was Mr. Custer borrowing a robe that hour of the night when he should've been fast asleep? Mrs. Spencer?"

She turns her head and stares at me. "He used to go down to the kitchen and steal streusel buns when the bakery van delivered."

"You telling me he'd go creeping around in the wee hours of the morning, risk having the management come down on him, just for some streusel buns?"

She looks at me with this terrible disdain. "You ever get up in the middle of the night, want something to eat, make yourself a cup of cocoa?"

"Sure."

"It's no big deal, is it?"

"Well, no."

"Wait and see. If the day comes when you can't just get up and make yourself a cup of cocoa any hour of the day or night, you'll see how a hunger can grow."

"I'm sorry I'm so dumb," I says.

Her eyes tear up a little bit. She shakes her head and says, "That's all right. Funny thing about life. I know how it feels to be as old as you, but you don't know what it feels like to be as old as me."

"So, Mrs. Spencer," I says, "was the streusel buns the only reason Mr. Custer crept out of his room naked and come to you for a bathrobe?"

"He wanted to make a phone call."

"To who?"

"To you."

"Why to me?"

"Because he knew you were Mr. Delvin's friend, and he'd heard them talking."

"Heard who talking?"

"He wouldn't say. He told me it was better I didn't know."

"What were these people talking about?"

"How long Mr. Delvin would last and how it had to look like an accident like before."

"Before what?"

"I don't know. Just before."

"Anything else?"

"One of them said they'd better take their time because this little Irishman with a long nose was sniffing around, but if they played the game right they'd have the suspicious little bastard as a witness to his friend Delvin's slow decline. Or maybe he'd do what most people did and give up visiting after a while and then they could just go ahead and do it and not have to worry."

"Whooosh," I says.

"Then one of them asked the other one if the business with the new will was all taken care of. That's what Charlie Custer told me."

"Why didn't you tell somebody?"

"Who was I going to tell? Charlie wouldn't say who he'd overheard. I walk up and tell somebody, I could be telling one of the wrong people."

"You could've told me."

She looks at me a long time before she says, "You're not old yet. Just wait and see. Nobody listens to you most of the time. If they do, they treat you like a child. They think half of what you say is nonsense and the other half lies. Nobody pays attention, just you wait and see."

"I'm paying attention."

"Do you think I would've been smart to bet on that? You could've just as easy gone and talked to someone about what I'm telling you, and then how would I've protected myself? You can't protect yourself very well when you grow old." She reaches out and touches my hand. "Just you wait and see," she says again.

I give her a kiss on the cheek.

"You ever need me, all you got to do is ask," I says.

I walk over to the desk, looking back once at Agnes Spencer, but she's looking at the television again, waiting for the young woman to arrive who'll take her on probably the first outing she's had in a long, long time.

"How you there, Mistuh Flannery? Come to see your fren'?" St. John asks me.

"How is he?"

"I ain' heard no complaints."

"Had a good night's sleep, did he?"

He frowns, wondering why I'm pushing these silly questions at him. Wondering if I'm pulling in the net so I can unload something on him. "I suppose he did. I'm working days. You can see."

So nobody even knows Delvin's missing yet, I think.

"You got a minute for a couple of questions?"

"Questions abou' what?"

"About your shoes. When I found Mr. Custer's body I didn't see no size-thirteen footprints around the pond and under the bushes. But after we left you watching the body and after the cops arrive, they find prints."

"So, I walk aroun' a little. Dat old dead man makes me nervous."

"I don't think so. I don't think there's much can make you nervous."

He grins, showing me what a bold hero he is.

"Except I can make you nervous."

"How's dat?"

"I got a little clout here and there. I drop a word and maybe the immigration comes look you over. You want to make a bet?"

"What kind of bet?"

"Five'll get you twenty you're an illegal. What do you say?"

"I'm going home soon anyhow," he says.

"Got your bundle? Made enough to be a prince of the island? Immigration takes a look at you, they take a look at your finances, too. You don't jump aboard a plane, a boat, with a pocket full of money. Now, you want to tell me why you was crawling around under the bushes by the duck pond?"

He reaches into his pocket and comes out with his hand closed around something.

"I see this," he says, and he opens his hand.

There's a plastic pen lying on his palm. One of them novelty pens with a lady on it what loses her bathing suit when you turn her upside down.

# 36

After supper I go over to the house where Murray Rourke still lives with his mother and father.

It's a Catholic house with a picture of Christ wearing the crown of thorns in the parlor along with a plaster statue of St. Anthony sitting on a table with some plastic flowers around its feet. Also a family Bible big enough to weight down the corner of a canvas tent in a high wind.

Rourke either reads my mind or sees where my eyes go when he ushers me into the living room.

"My mother," he says.

"Thank God the women keep the faith," I says by way of being polite. "And where is she? I'd like to pay my respects."

"Out at the bingo in the church basement."

"Thank God for bingo," I says, making a little joke.

He grins, giving me the courtesy of acting like he thinks what I said was funny. "God bless the sinners."

"And the father?" I asks, wondering why the hell we're talking like a couple of harps from the old country.

"Having a few with the boys down to the tavern."

There it is, the old Irish family ritual, Pop down at the tavern having a few with the boys and Ma at church—even if it is the bingo in the church basement.

192

"Will you have . . . You don't drink, do you, Jimmy? I almost forgot," Rourke says.

"You go ahead," I says.

"I don't need it. I could pour you a cup of tea. Ma left a pot."

"I've just had my supper, thank you kindly, Murray. Had three cups of coffee. My back teeth are floating," I says, turning down his offer of hospitality the proper way, making a little story of it so feelings wouldn't be hurt.

He grins again and says, "Well, you can go into the toilet and have a pee."

"I'll take you up on that, if I feel an urgency," I says.

"So sit down, then, and rest your feet," he says, sitting down hisself. "What can I do you for, Jimmy?"

"You can tell me who you called from Evergreen's office the other night over to the Larkspur Nursing Home."

The last trace of the grin disappears, and his eyes go flat. For a second I'm afraid I'm going to see a little of the monster that Rourke can let out whenever it suits him. But he takes a breath and lets it out, turning his head away while he gets himself under control.

"That's a hell of a question to be asking me. I could've been calling a girlfriend. I could've been calling my bookie."

"Well, you could. I suppose you could be calling a girlfriend or a bookie at three, four o'clock in the morning, but somehow, I don't think you was."

"So the call could've been official. And if it was official, a civilian's got no right to be asking a law enforcement officer who he was calling."

"I ain't asking as a civilian."

"What, then?"

"A friend. A friend of almost fifteen years."

He lets out a gust of air like he's been holding the breath he took when he turned his head and reached out to put his hand on the Bible lying on the table.

"You know what I think?" I says after a while.

"What do you think, Jimmy?"

"I think you put in a call to somebody in the city government or somebody in the party."

"What would I do that for, Jimmy?"

"To tell them there was another old person dead under suspicious circumstances at the nursing home. To ask them how you was supposed to handle it."

"Nobody had to tell O'Shea and me how to handle it. We know how to handle a death by misadventure."

"I don't think it was an accident, Murray."

"What makes you say that?"

"Mr. Custer told Mrs. Spencer he wanted to borrow her bathrobe so he could call me and tell me something."

"Like you say, Jimmy, at three, four o'clock in the morning?"

"What other chance could the old man get if he thought somebody was keeping an eye on him? Also I heard a door slam down the street when I found the body."

"Jesus, Mary, and Joseph," he says, dipping his head in respect, "what's a car door slamming tell you?"

"It tells me that somebody could've been visiting Evergreen at the Larkspur and maybe overheard the old man making the call to me and . . ."

I let it trail off. Rourke would fill in the rest.

"Visiting Evergreen?" he says.

"She was wearing black stockings and a garter belt."

"She don't look the type."

"Well, I don't know what's the type. That's what she was wearing under her robe, and she was up at that hour."

"Having a little wrestle with that buck from Trinidad."

"Oh, that's what she was willing to let us think. And that's what he was willing to let us think. Her because she figured we wouldn't look no farther for some other man. Him because it gave him a lever for all sorts of favors."

"So what do you figure was the personal time he was taking?"

I shrug my shoulders. "I don't know every answer to every question. There's some good-looking young women working in that place. Maybe he was getting his while Evergreen was getting hers."

"That's it?"

I take out the novelty pen and hand it to Rourke.

"What's this?"

"A novelty like the kind of novelties Francis Carmody sells in wholesale lots. St. John found it under the bushes by the pond. That's how come he left his footprints. Picking it up."

"There could be pens like this scattered all over Chicago."

"It's a brand-new item," I says.

"How come we didn't find Carmody's footprints under the bush?" he asks.

"I'm working on that," I says.

"It's not much to take to the district attorney," he says.

"It's nothing. I know that."

"The call I made was to Wally Dunleavy," Rourke says.

"How come?"

"After the Feltons died like they did, the investigations didn't go nowhere."

"Pressure from above?"

"Nothing heavy. No big deal. Special Crimes just turned it over to Senior Citizens' Services. When O'Shea and me kept nosing around a little on our own, we were just told they'd been booked as death by misadventure and to stop wasting our time."

"How did Dunleavy come into it?"

"He gave me a call one day and asked me to give him a call if there was ever another accidental death at Larkspur."

"He said give him a call at four in the morning?"

"He said any hour."

"So that's what you did and didn't even wonder why?"

"He asked the favor, Jimmy. You know how—"

"Sure, I know how that goes, Murray. When you do a favor for a favor, you don't ask the reason why."

# 37

I go over to see Dunleavy at Streets and Sanitation again.

He greets me with the usual, "Hello there, you're Mike Flannery's kid, ain't you?"

"Mr. Dunleavy," I says, "I been coming to see you, now and then, for the last fifteen, twenty years. Every time I walk through the door you say the same thing like you've got to really stretch to remember my name. I wonder why you do that."

He knows I'm out to challenge him about something, but he don't know what, so he just gives me the old one-eye and says, "So why do you think I do that?"

"I think it's a habit you got into. Like the old horse traders who made believe they didn't know which end of the horse you was supposed to feed and which end you was supposed to sweep up after. It gives you an edge."

"What kind of an edge?"

"It makes the other person grateful you remembered him when you're such a busy man, with so many people of your acquaintance, that you could be expected to forget a person who might think they was insignificant."

"Do you think you're insignificant?"

"I don't think anybody's insignificant, Mr. Dunleavy."

"So is this a complaint you're filing concerning our relation-ship?"

"No, sir. It's just an observation. Like I never know you to give half an answer. Either you know what you're talking about and speak right up or you won't say nothing until you got all the facts."

"You got a point," he says, making it a statement, not a question.

"The other day when I asked you about Mr. Delvin's cousin you was vague about the relationship."

"Give me a break, will you, Flannery? How am I supposed to know is this Carmody a second cousin twice removed or a third cousin through marriage?"

"That's just what I'm saying. If you didn't know for sure, you would've said nothing."

He takes off his eyeglasses, folds them, and puts them into his pocket. I don't know if that means he's ready to settle down to a long conversation or if he's showing me a bare face as a token of his honesty.

"You can sure make boils out of pimples," he says.

"Let me put it another way, Mr. Dunleavy. If somebody asks you a question like that about somebody and you don't have the information, I know you have your people dig into it and you have the information pretty damn quick. So what've you found out about Francis Carmody?"

"Roseann, Delvin's grandmother on his mother's side, had five children by her fourth husband, Aloysius Flynn. Clara, the eldest, married Chip's father, Martin Delvin. The youngest, Belle, mar-ried Michael Carmody. Belle and Mike were Francis Carmody's grandparents. Their boy, William Carmody, was Carmody's fa-ther. So you figure out what that makes Chips Delvin to Francis Carmody."

"That's almost exactly word for word what Carmody rattled off to me," I says.

"You pride yourself on your memory, too, do you, Flannery?"

"Some things stick when they got a reason to stick."

"And what reason have you got for anything about this Carmody to stick in your busy brain?"

"He's around both times when Mr. and Mrs. Felton die by accident. I think he maybe was around when Mr. Custer drowned in the duck pond. He's a guy with no past to speak of."

"What makes you say that?"

"He seems to know a lot of politicians, and I don't know him. I never heard of him before."

"You don't know everybody, Flannery."

"I think I'd know somebody who was recommended for a public-service job by three heavyweights like Jack Reddy, Dr. Henry Perkanola, and Wally Dunleavy, Superintendent of Streets and Sanitation."

His eyes go flat on me.

I don't want to make an enemy, I just want to know a little bit of the truth.

"I'm not yelling political corruption here, Mr. Dunleavy. I'm just asking you how the arrangement comes about."

"All right. About a year ago this Carmody comes to me one day handing out these little souvenirs, plastic key chains, plastic dog poop, rulers with inscriptions on them like "Vote for Aces Malone for a Fair Measure." Like that. I tell him I'm not in the market. He's got the wrong man. I ain't the purchasing agent for the Democratic Party, and I ain't the campaign manager for anybody running for office. He says all he's doing is going around making friends. So I send him over to Delvin to make friends with him. I figure that way I get rid of a pest."

"Where does this second cousin twice removed business get started?"

"I give him the names and the background. I draw him the tree."

"What for? What's that supposed to do?"

"You understand favor for favor. You also understand get-back?"

"It's like you pull one on me and I pull one on you. Like them brothers I read about. One year one of them gives the other one a ton of elephant shit delivered on his front stoop for a birthday present. The next year he gets his back with a two-ton ice sculpture of a walrus melting on the living-room rug."

"That's right. You do to me and I do to you. Get-back. Old

Delvin and me've been doing get-back on each other ever since he stole Sheila Harrigan away at the Sons of Hibernia Annual Dance by telling her I had a dose of clap. We was eighteen, twenty. It's been going on ever since. So that's all it was. Just a little get-back. Just a little finger in Delvin's eye. A little something to bother him. I never expected him to believe this Carmody was his cousin, but maybe he wanted to think there was somebody out there with some of his blood in him. That when he went there'd be a little of it left behind."

"If that's all it was, how did it end up you and Reddy and Perkanola sponsor Carmody?"

"Delvin asked the favor. Why he asked the three of us I don't know. He could've picked any other three, I suppose."

"Or he could be pulling a get-back. We know he'd have reason to pull one on you. Maybe he had reason to pull one on Perkanola and Reddy, too."

"How the hell would he've worked that?"

"Who put you into Larkspur stock?"

"Carmody. After he started working as an ombudsman he came to me and told me Larkspur was one of the best-run facilities around and was sure to make money."

"And you didn't have somebody check it out?"

His eyes flick away from mine for a second, but I can read what was in them all the same. He's ashamed to tell me he got greedy and went for the bait without finding out was it a real worm on the hook. He's ashamed to admit he could've got taken in like some silly citizen sold a bill of goods by a smooth con merchant.

"You think Delvin would have any reason to pull get-backs on Perkanola and Reddy?"

"I don't know about Perkanola, but Reddy and Delvin've had at it in a friendly way more than once."

I'm trying to work it through. Maybe Dunleavy's also trying to work it through. Anyway, we're both sitting there quiet.

Finally I says, "So, like this, you play a little joke on Delvin by sending over a man who can claim to be his cousin and maybe unload a gross of pens on the old man. Delvin either falls for the story about being relations or don't fall for it. But one way or the other he gets you and Reddy and Perkanola to sponsor this no-account for ombudsman. You do it because you think Delvin's asking a favor for a cousin you manufactured and it's all part of the joke. But this Carmody gets you to invest in Larkspur."

"Also Perkanola and Reddy," Dunleavy says, like he wants to make it clear that he wasn't the only one got snookered.

"Maybe Delvin knew about that part of it, maybe he didn't. The point is, when the Feltons died under suspicious circumstances, Carmody got onto the three of you to ease off any investigations anybody, the police included, might get into. Otherwise the Fair Winds stock would go into the toilet."

"If I'd thought the Felton deaths were anything but accidents, Jimmy . . ."

I feel like saying he'd've probably done just like he did because he'd've convinced himself that here was these two old people were old, ready to die anyway, and he had his own old age to worry about.

That's the worst thing about getting old. It turns us into cowards because we figure there ain't going to be anybody around to take care of us if we don't do it for ourselves.

"So what we got here," I says, "is a little get-back making get-backs on top of get-backs, and everybody ends up stepping in it."

"Stepping into what, Jimmy?" Dunleavy asks.

"Extortion, maybe. Fraud, maybe. Even murder, maybe."

# 38

Carmody's got an office on the second floor of an old building on a rundown block along Washington.

My heels make a lot of noise on the old wooden floor of the hallway, bouncing off the walls, adding to a racket of voices coming from behind a door halfway down. I can't make out all the words, all I can get is pieces and the fact that one voice is a man's and the other a woman's.

"... ahead with it!" the woman says.

"... asking ... wait," the man says.

Then they stop short like they sense somebody's coming up to the door. I wait a second, listening like they're listening. The door opens and Carmody's standing there looking both ways down the hall. He sees me and frowns.

I hear a door close inside his office.

Carmody smiles. "You say something?"

"No."

"Must've come from one of the offices down the hall. Come on in." He holds the door open for me. I go in, taking a look at his name and the words "Manufacturer's Representative" painted on it in black letters edged with tarnished gold.

"Walls like paper in this building," he says.

At the back of his office there's a side door. I'm listening for footsteps going down the back stairs, but Carmody's covering up

201

any sounds like that with a cheery invitation to have a chair that's a lot bigger and friendlier than I got any right to expect.

Also he's shaking my hand and practically dragging me across the office to his desk. "I don't know to what I owe this pleasure, but I'm very glad you stopped by to see me. I've been hoping for another meeting."

"How's that?"

He sits down in his chair and picks up something off the desk. It's one of them little pens with the naked lady in it.

"I'm afraid we got off on the wrong foot the other day," he says. "You took me by surprise."

"You mean you didn't think Mr. Delvin had any friends that would come looking to see how he was doing?"

"No. I know that my cousin has hundreds of friends. Maybe thousands."

"But me and my old man, Mike, have been the only ones come to see him so far?"

He makes a sad face. "That's true. But I'm sure they'll get around to it. The point is that we—the two of us, you and me—have already demonstrated our concern, and there shouldn't be any quarrel between us."

"How come you don't tell me you're the ombudsman from the citizens' watchdog committee what's keeping an eye on the Larkspur?" I asks.

He fiddles with the pen a little faster. I can't help looking at it.

"Well, like I say," he says, "you rubbed me the wrong way for some reason, and I didn't feel I had any obligation to tell you."

"Well, I was there making threats—I understand that—which was all the more reason to tell me who you were, just to shut me up, if for no other reason."

"That's what I should've done. I admit that. So now you've given me the chance to explain."

"Maybe you can explain how come the reports you put in started out bad and ended up good."

His eyebrows go up.

"I had lunch with Mrs. Blalock," I says.

"I've got to hand it to you, Flannery, once you get a hold on something, you don't let go."

"So what's the answer?"

"You didn't see the place before Lenore Evergreen took over, did you?"

"No."

"It was a snake pit. She's making a difference. I wanted to give her a chance to turn the place around."

"That why you put Delvin in there?"

"Partly. I wanted to show Ms. Evergreen that I was willing to back her up with more than nice words and good intentions. Also Larkspur's on my rounds, so I could check up on my cousin at the same time I inspected Larkspur."

"Kill two birds with one stone?"

"Well, that's not the nicest way of putting it."

I give him a smile to encourage him.

He takes a breath and gives me a nice smile back.

We're like a couple of dogs showing our teeth, pretending to be friendly, careful as hell seeing that the other one don't get the first bite.

"So they're doing better?"

"I think so."

"Less bugs? Less rats? Less lousy food? Less pissy sheets?"

"I think so."

"But not less people dying by misadventure."

He just stares at me.

Finally he says, "We're all trying to do our best."

I get up like I'm ready to go.

"Is that all you wanted to see me about?" he says.

"Oh, there's one other thing," I says. "You could refresh my memory."

"What's that?" he says.

"How'd you say your relationship with Delvin works?"

"Roseann, Frank's grandmother on her mother's side, had five children by her fourth husband, Aloysius Flynn. Clara, the eldest, married Frank's father, Martin Delvin. The youngest, Belle, married Michael Carmody. Belle and Mike were my grandparents. Their son, William Carmody, was my father."

"That's what I thought you told me before. Word for word. That's what Wally Dunleavy told me, too. I had a cup of coffee with him."

He fiddles with the pen even faster. He's done something criminal, and he knows I've got him.

"Hey, the pen you gave me ran out of ink the first time I tried to use it," I says.

"That's okay. I only got three samples, and I'm not going to order any. You take a look at it? It's a novelty that hasn't got much of a chance."

He hands it over to me, and I look at it really close for the first time. The face on the little naked lady is the face of a well-known ex-mayor who lost for another try at the job last time out.

I start to hand it back, and he says, "Keep it. Anything else takes your fancy, all you've got to do is say the word."

"You got one for yourself? It could be a collector's item someday."

"I gave the third one to Jeannie Felton. I wanted to see if it'd make her blush." He waves his hand at me, showing me how generous he is. "But that's all right. Keep it. Keep it."

I walk out of his office without saying anything, figuring I'll just let him stew about what I mean to do.

I cross the street and turn the corner. Then I duck back against the wall and wait a minute.

I'm hoping that whoever it was having the argument with Carmody when my footsteps on the wood warned them somebody was coming would come back to finish what she had to say. I'm pretty sure that whoever it was is going to turn out to be Lenore Evergreen.

I peek around the corner, and sure enough there's a woman just about to step back into the building. She's got the leavings of her argument with Carmody still on her face. But even so she looks like the princess off the page of a book of fairy tales. It ain't Lenore Evergreen. It's Jeannie Felton.

I hang around maybe twenty minutes until she comes out again. She's got a smile on her face, so I figure they settled any differences between them in the second go-round.

I follow her down the block to a parking lot, where she gets into a trim little red convertible BMW. Probably something she bought for herself out of the ten thousand her aunt left her.

I leg it back to my old Chevy, get in, and pull a U, dropping right behind her before she's half a block down the avenue.

I tail her into Uptown, not the best section of the neighborhood but the worst. She pulls in at the curb around the middle of the block, in front of a six-flat trying to look respectable with everything decaying and falling down around it. I park on the corner.

There's an old woman picking through a Dumpster sitting there at the curb like somebody'd just forgot it or tossed it away along with the garbage it's got in it. She looks up when Jeannie calls to her and waves her over. I see her pass the old woman a bill and point to the BMW. She holds up two fingers. I don't have to be close enough to hear that she's asking the bag lady to keep an eye on her vehicle while she goes inside for a couple of minutes.

Once she's through the front door I take a quick walk down the street and into the vestibule. The mailboxes have been torn open long ago, but there's still a couple of printed cards in the nameplates. One of them says "F. Carmody."

I go back to my car. The old woman's giving me the old one-eye and spreading her arms like she's ready to keep me from doing damage to the BMW's shiny paint job.

Jeannie Felton comes out a half a minute later with a jacket on a hanger in a plastic cleaner's bag in her hand.

I follow her again.

This time she drives to a high rise on Lake Shore Drive West in Lincoln Park. This vestibule don't have any busted mailboxes. In fact, it don't have any at all, because it's got a porter to take care of such things. But there's a line of nameplates and bell buttons set into the marble wall of the vestibule so visitors can announce themselves and get buzzed through when there's no porter on duty.

When I look through the window in the inside door I can see the day man escorting Jeannie back to the elevators carrying the jacket. Which gives me time enough to run my finger down the line of nameplates. There's no J. Felton by itself, but there's a J. Felton and an F. Carmody with a slash separating them.

It's interesting to me that her name should be first.

I decide to hang around and see if she comes out again. It's warm in the car, and I doze off.

When I wake up, maybe two hours've gone by. I figure she's probably already gone if she was going out again, or she's upstairs and ain't going anywhere. So I might as well go home.

Then I see this lady come out of the front door.

At first I don't even recognize her. This ain't no porcelain pastel doll. This ain't no marzipan puppet on a wedding cake. This is a lady with her hair slicked back and pinned with a jeweled clip, silver slippers on her feet, and a lamé gown hugging her like the skin on a snake. This is a lady into glamour. This is a lady into power. This is a lady into money. This is Jeannie Felton.

I don't bother tailing her anymore. I don't really think it matters where she's going.

I wander over to the apartment house.

The doorman's standing in the doorway enjoying the breeze that's kicking up off the lake.

Like the guys what work in the sewers know practically every other guy what works in the sewers, I notice that practically every doorman working these luxury apartment houses knows practically every other doorman working them.

"Nice night," I says.

He fingers the patent-leather brim on his cap and says, "Yes, sir."

"Does Danny Maroon still work here?" I asks.

"When was this?"

"Oh, three, four years ago."

"No Danny Maroon worked here three, four years ago. There's a Danny Maroon works in a building down the Drive, maybe a mile, maybe a mile and a half."

"That's got to be him. How many Danny Maroons could there be? He's a hell of a nice guy."

"Good poker player," the doorman says.

"You play with him much?"

"Now and then."

"I used to sit in on a game."

"Three, four years ago?"

"About that."

"So how come you don't know he never worked here?"

I look around like I'm impressed by the place. "Hey, all these fancy anthills look the same to me."

"I know what you mean."

"That was some looker what just trotted out of here."

He shrugs and makes a little face.

"You know something?"

"I shouldn't say."

"Well, if you can't, I understand. You work for these rich people, you're afraid to open your mouth."

"I ain't afraid to open my mouth."

"I didn't mean that exactly."

"I don't know if Miss Felton's rich."

"She's a miss? Don't tell me she's a working girl!"

"You mean a *sex*retary?" he says, wiggling his eyebrows.

"Well, living in a place like this."

"She don't live alone."

"Sharing with a girlfriend?"

"Boyfriend."

"That explains it."

"I don't know if that explains it," he says. "The manager tells me she took the lease out in her own name. Paid first, last, and security. Now it's three months, and she's only paid the rent for one and a half."

"Uh-oh."

"That's right."

So maybe, I think, the BMW and the apartment was bought on expectations, but the fruit didn't fall into her lap.

"It's been nice talking to you," I says.

"Any time."

"Say hello to Danny Maroon the next time you play cards," I says.

"Who'll I say?"

"Jimmy Flannery."

"Well, I'll be damned. Maroon talks about you all the time. You was the guy what found a home for Baby, the gorilla, when the furnace at the zoo broke down. Also you found the guy what was chewed in half by the alligator."

That's what it means to be famous in Chicago.

# 39

The next morning I sleep a little late, but I'm still up before Mary because she's still on nights. I go out into the kitchen to make myself some breakfast. I give Alfie a little breakfast, too. Then he wants to go for a walk. So I do that to kill some time because I decide I'm going to take the day off.

We take a walk over to Horan Park, and I stand there in the early morning light looking at the lot where our house would've been. I don't know if I'm doing the right thing about that.

I don't know if I'm doing the right thing about a lot of things.

I'm wondering if they found Delvin missing over to the Larkspur yet. The way they run that place it's possible nobody would even know he wasn't in his bed more than twenty-four hours after I got him out of there. Or maybe they know and Evergreen's keeping it quiet because that's all they need is an old man missing after another old man drowned in the duck pond.

I'm thinking about how I should be feeling more comfortable what with Delvin safe at my flat. But something keeps nagging and nagging at me. I can't put my finger on it.

Alfie and me stroll back to the house. It's almost nine o'clock. I go upstairs. Mary's still sleeping.

I decide to do some figuring about what it could cost to buy the building and remodel all the apartments. I get a piece of paper and I grab a pen out the pocket of my jacket. It don't write. It's the pen what gave up on me over to the Water Service Bureau. I go to the jacket again. I got Duke the Plumber's pen and the other novelty pen what Carmody gave me when I was over to his office.

Then it hits me.

He had three pens.

He gives me two.

He gives the other one to Jeannie Felton.

So, if he's telling the truth, it wasn't him what dropped the pen under the bush near Mr. Custer's body.

It was Jeannie Felton. The lady what looks like Alice in Wonderland during the day and Marilyn Monroe at night. The angel of mercy what was taking Mrs. Spencer, who had a conversation with Mr. Custer just before he was killed and wanders around every chance she gets just like he used to try to do, on a boat ride on the lake this morning. At ten o'clock this morning.

It's ten-ten by the kitchen clock.

I tell Alfie I'll be back and run down the stairs. I kick over the old Chevy and peel rubber getting away from the curb. I drive like hell to the Dan Ryan Expressway, down to Sixty-third, over to Cornell Drive in the park, and up to the place where they rent the paddle boats.

The kid there remembers the pretty young blonde with the nice old lady. I ask him what they was wearing.

"They both had on summer dresses with flowers," the kid says. "The young one had on a floppy hat, and the old one had one of them umbrellas for the sun."

I ask him which way they went out on the lagoon, and he says they went paddling south.

I stand there wondering which I should do, rent a paddle boat or run around the shore.

"You want to rent a boat?" the kid asks.

I start to run. The ground's very uneven in places. There's bushes and willows growing right down to the water. There's a lot of people out on the lagoon in the paddle boats. Every once in a while I stop and look out, trying to spot Mrs. Spencer and Jeannie. I figure I got a chance with one of them in a big hat and one of them holding a parasol over her head.

Every time I stop, I don't see them. At least, I don't think I see them. It worries me I could be looking right at them and, what with the reflections off the water, I might not know it was them.

Then I think what a dope I am looking out in the middle of the lagoon. If Jeannie Felton's out to do Mrs. Spencer in, she'll find herself a nice secluded nook at the side near the shore. Under some trees. Where nobody can see.

So I keep running. There's the west lagoon and the east lagoon. There's an awful lot of lagoon to run around. After five, ten minutes I'm panting like an old dog who can't hunt no more. I'm sorry I didn't take my old man up on his offer to go running with him long ago.

I'm just about ready to stop for a minute—it ain't going to do Mrs. Spencer any good if I drop dead from a heart attack—when I hear somebody crying for help and a lot of splashing around. It's a woman's voice, muffled but nearby.

I keep running right through a stand of trees and bushes by the water's edge at this little bend in the shore like a cup.

Mrs. Spencer's out about thirty yards. Jeannie Felton's standing up in the paddle boat watching her drown. Then she hears somebody yell, and she turns around to see a couple of young guys in a paddle boat coming around the bend about two hundred yards out.

"Hang on dear, I'll save you," she hollers, and she jumps in the water.

I don't think she means to save Mrs. Spencer. She means to make sure she drowns before the two guys can reach them. She's probably thinking how it's lucky they came along. Now she's got witnesses that it was an accident and that she tried to do her best to save the old woman.

I don't really feel like a swim after all that running, but there's nothing else I can do. I jump in.

Jeannie hears me thrashing through the water while she's trying to hold the old lady down. She turns her head and sees me coming.

First she looks surprised, and then she looks like she wishes it was me she was pushing under the water.

I reach her and tear her off Mrs. Spencer. She tries to fight back, but I hit her one and she backs off. Then she gives it up altogether and starts swimming to the shore. I can't go after her because I got to get Mrs. Spencer out of there.

By the time I drag her up on the grass, Jeannie Felton's running down through the park, and the young guys in the paddle boat are still trying to reach us.

"Why'd Jeannie try to drown me?" Mrs. Spencer says, sitting there on the grass looking like a drowned kitten. "I was going to leave her all my money because she was so good to me."

"I didn't know you had any money," I says.

She gives me the old one-eye and says, "That's why I got it."

I lie there next to her puffing like an old wore-out steam locomotive.

"Well," she says after a while, "ain't you going to go after her?"

"I'll call it in to the cops. They'll get her. She's got no place to go."

# 40

Lenore Evergreen's looking very fragile. She's sitting there in the parlor of the Larkspur clutching her blouse at the throat. I notice she ain't wearing any black stockings. I'm willing to bet she ain't wearing no garter belt either.

"I'm to blame, you know," she says.

"How do you figure that?"

"I thought I could dazzle everybody. I thought I could come in here as director and do a better job than any man'd been able to do. I was going to show them. The job was too big for me, and I wouldn't admit it."

"It was too big for anybody," I says. "You was doing the best you could."

She looks at me like what I just said makes her angry. "That's the song every incompetent do-gooder's sung from the beginning of time. It's not enough to want to do the right thing. You've got to be ready to bite the bullet. Blow the whistle. Cry for help. Admit you can't pick up the goddam stone all by yourself."

I don't say anything. She wants to beat herself, let her beat herself. Sometimes that makes people feel better.

She glares at me. "You knew I was a phony," she says.

"Well, no, I didn't," I says. "I thought you was a murderer or at least a conspirator."

Her face does a number and ends up looking dumbfounded.

"When I came to the door with the news of Mr. Custer's body, I saw you was wearing black stockings. Later on, when you took a tumble after looking at Mr. Custer's face, I saw you was wearing some pretty fancy underwear."

Her face has colored up like she's got a fever.

"My God, Flannery, you know everything about me, don't you?"

"No, I don't. I just know what I saw with my own eyes."

"And you figured the dumpy little Ms. Evergreen was living a hot and heavy night life. And if she was doing that, she could be conspiring to do a little evil. Tapping the till. Killing off old people for the money they'd leave to Larkspur, where I could get my hands on it."

I don't say yes, I don't say no. I just look at her like it's okay with me if she tells the story.

"Dichotomy, Flannery. Do you know what dichotomy is?"

"Sure. One part of me wanted to build a house on the lot Mrs. Banjo left me, and another part of me didn't want it at all."

"Did you make up your mind about what you were going to do?"

"It was kind of made up for me. Circumstances decided it."

"Handy things, circumstances. I wish circumstances could decide my life for me. One part of me wants to be the big corporate success. Another part of me wants to be a wife, or at least somebody's love. But so far I haven't been lucky. No lover in a three-piece suit driving a late-model car has come my way."

"Three-piece suit in a late-model car?" I says.

She smiles for the first time since I got there to tell her it was me took Delvin out of Larkspur. "Okay, Flannery," she says, making her voice rough and bawdy, "a stud in tight jeans riding a Harley. Hell, if a lady's going to have fantasies, she might as well go the whole hog."

"So that's all it was, just playing dress-up?"

"That's all. The funny thing is, I was ready to have you and everybody believe I was having it off with the help rather than admit that I was night-dreaming like a teenager."

"We all got to have our dreams. I got a couple of other things bothering me."

She raises her eyebrows and waits for the questions.

"How come you went directly to the duck pond when I told you I'd found a body?"

She shrugs her shoulders. "I don't know," she says. "Maybe because I always had the feeling there'd be some tragedy around—or because of—that silly thing."

"And how come you got faint and fell over like you did when you saw it was Mr. Custer? I had the idea it was because you expected it to be somebody else."

"For God's sake, Flannery. I may have seen a lot since I've been in this business, but I never saw a man's hair and scalp nibbled out by ducks before. Now I want you to answer a couple of questions for me."

"Go ahead."

"Who is this Francis Carmody?"

"Just a hustler who got handed a chance."

"When did he start living with Jeannie Felton?"

"After she decided she could use him more ways than one."

"She killed her aunt and uncle?"

"For their money. But they didn't leave it to her."

"And she was going to kill Mrs. Spencer for her money, too?"

"Looks that way."

"How'd she expect to get away with it?"

"Why not? She got away with it three times before. Carmody's selling Dunleavy, Reddy, Perkanola, and a lot of other big shots on Fair Wind stock produced an unexpected bonus for her own schemes. She was protected because they were protecting their investment."

"Was she planning to do in your Mr. Delvin?"

"She was feeding him slow poison. She figured Delvin would leave his money—at least some of it—to his only living relative. And she and Carmody were living together by then."

"What about Mr. Custer? He didn't have a dime. He was welfare."

"He had information. He was always on the eary, and he heard Carmody and Felton talking things over about Delvin, only he thought he was listening to Carmody and you."

She gives a little gasp. So now she figures that's her fault, too.

I know there's nothing I can say to change her mind about that. She's going to have to work it out for herself.

"Mr. Custer told her about his suspicions and how he meant to call and warn me, Delvin's friend. So she came back in the small hours and unlocked his door so he could steal some streusel buns. Everybody knew what a sweet tooth he had. The only thing she forgot was to bring him something to wear, so he had to go get a robe from Mrs. Spencer so he could make the call. Jeannie Felton was waiting for him."

From down the hall that woman yells out, "You sons of bitches, let me loose. A person can't even scratch her ass when she's got an itch. Wait'll Jake gets here. For Christ's sake, Jake, where are you?"

# 41

Delvin's not on the couch. He ain't been on the couch for ten days. He's lying in my bed acting like an emperor holding court for all his political cronies. All the drugs is out of his system, so he's no more ga-ga than he usually is.

Mary, Mike, and me are sitting in the kitchen.

"I'm going in there and tell him he's got to find other accommodations," I says. "This is getting to be too much, him kicking Mary and me out of our own bed."

"He didn't kick us out, James," Mary says, holding herself in because she wants to be charitable, wants to be fair. "We volunteered to give up our bed for a few nights after all the old man's been through."

"You bounced him around like a rubber ball," Mike says in Delvin's defense.

"To save his life."

"Even so, you might've found a way that was easier on the old fella."

"So now it's like I'm responsible for him for the rest of his life?"

"That's the way it is amongst the Chinese. You save somebody's life, you're responsible for him forever."

"Well, I ain't going to do it. It's time for him to go home."

"I don't know if we can send him home to an empty house,

James," Mary says, "and he says he just won't pay for private nurses. He's made that very clear."

I smile, but before Mary or Mike can ask me what I got up my sleeve the phone rings, and I go to answer it.

While I'm talking on the phone the front doorbell rings, and Mary gets up to go answer it.

When she comes back I'm off the phone, and I ask her who was at the door.

"Mr. Dunleavy, come to call on Mr. Delvin. Who was that on the phone?"

"Good news for you and me."

I hold up my finger, telling Mike and Mary that I'll give them the news in a minute. I leave the kitchen and go down the hall to the bedroom.

Dunleavy's sitting in a chair by the bed. Delvin's lying back against the pillows, smiling like a shark, showing his false teeth like he's ready to rip out Dunleavy's throat. I hide myself behind the door jamb so I can listen in without being seen. I can see them through the crack between the door and wall.

Dunleavy's doing the talking.

"I swear on my wife and mother's grave—"

"God rest their souls," Delvin says.

"—that it was meant to be a little joke. A scheme. A get-back. Who'd've ever dreamed that Carmody would've turned it into a confidence game against us?"

"To hell with the confidence game against you and the rest of the greedy buggers that're supposed to be my friends. What about—"

"You'd have done the same if you saw the chance to make a profit," Dunleavy manages to stick in edgeways.

But Delvin don't act like he even hears the remark, he just goes on. "—the murder game? That false cousin you saddled me with and that whey-faced twit of a girl who had him by the pecker was going to do me in."

"Whoever would've thought, Chips? Whoever would've thought? You think I'd ever pull a get-back on you what would actually endanger your life?" He reaches out his old-man's hand and lays it on Delvin's old-man's hand.

It squeezes my heart.

"For the good Lord's sake, Chips, you and me are just about the last of the strong young men we once was. Just you and me," Dunleavy says in the softest voice.

"So I guess we're stuck with each other, ain't we?" Delvin says.

"I guess so," Dunleavy says, hardly able to hide the glint in his eye that tells me he's congratulating himself on conning Delvin once again.

"So run along now, Wally. I know you got work to do," Delvin says.

Dunleavy gets up and shakes Delvin's hand.

"But one thing."

"What's that?"

"Keep one eye open, and count your change. You got a get-back coming from me, and it could land on you any day."

I clear my throat and walk into the room like I just arrived.

"Good to see you, Mr. Dunleavy," I says.

"Likewise, I'm sure, Jimmy. I hear you've decided to buy this old building and remodel all the apartments."

"With Mr. Delvin's generous help, that's the plan," I says.

"A lovely thought," Dunleavy says. "If you need me to grease the skids obtaining the various licenses and permits, all you got to do is say the word."

He gives me his hand to let me know he's giving me his word, and after saying he can find his way out, he tips a salute to Delvin and goes on his way.

"Good news," I says, turning to Delvin.

"What's that?"

"I know how eager you've been to get back to your own house and bed."

"Aye. When I'm able."

"I expect you'd be able right now if only you had a house-keeper."

"One that's suitable, of course," he says, letting me know by his pious expression that he's ready to make sacrifices in my behalf.

"I just got off the phone from Mrs. Thimble. You remember Mrs. Thimble. She was old Father Mulrooney's housekeeper."

"I thought she disappeared after the old priest died."

"I found her a place for her retirement run by the Catholic Church. But she tells me she's not happy there. Not enough to do. She's ready, willing, and able to start work for you on Monday."

"Who made her the offer?"

"Well, I did, Mr. Delvin. She's a fine woman what don't like cats, and I doubt you'll find better in all Chicago."

He's ready to tell me to go to hell and mind my own business, that he'll interview and hire his own housekeeper. But I cock my head a little and give him the old one-eye, reminding him that I saved his life and he owes me very large. He's got to pay off. It's the way it works.

Favor for favor.